The Roseate
Spoonbill of
Happiness

The Roseate Spoonbill of Happiness

Stories by
Marilyn Gear Pilling

BOHEME PRESS

Previous versions of some of these stories have appeared in Prairie
Fire, Room of One's Own, On the Threshold: Writing Toward the
Year 2000 (Beach Holme), Carousel, and Prism International.

Canadian Cataloguing in Publication Data

Pilling, Marilyn Gear
The roseate spoonbill of happiness

ISBN 1-894498-10-0

1. Women–Fiction. I. Title.

PS8581.I365R68 2002   C813'.54   C2002-900554-X
PR9199.3.P4965R68 2002

The publisher gratefully acknowledges the Canada Council
for the Arts for its support of our publishing program.

The Canada Council │ Le Conseil des Arts
for the Arts │ du Canada

Boheme Press
192 Spadina Avenue, Suite 308
Toronto, Ontario, Canada M5T 2C2
www.bohemeonline.com

This book is dedicated with love
to Sheena and Meredith Pilling
and to T. W. McKergow

"Once, in Union, Maine, as we were passing
a field, five white birch trees became five white
ponies. Their feet shuffled in the long grass, their
white faces shone. This is called: happiness."

— Mary Oliver, *Winter Hours*

Table of Contents

The Roseate Spoonbill of Happiness

Objects of happiness are always round.
Happiness rounds out everything it enters.
— *Gaston Bachelard*

*W*hen my daughter returned from Japan, I saw that she had changed in her forearms and in her fingers. When I told people this, they laughed, not as if I had said something funny, but as if I had said something weird.

I understood this reaction. The forearms are an unremarked part of the body. One never hears, "he married her for her forearms" as one might hear, "he married her for her hair." And fingers are fingers, not thought of as susceptible to change.

One neighbour laughed and moved the conversation quickly away from my weirdness. "It must be wonderful to have your daughter home again," she said.

"It is wonderful," I told her, speaking intensely. "After she was born, I would wake up in the morning feeling happy in a fundamental way. The happiness was that she existed, that she was here, in this world." I was leaning forward into my taken-aback neighbour's space. "Since she's returned from Japan, I've been surprised by this same happiness every morning. For an instant, when I wake up, the bluebird of happiness is sitting on my chest. No," I shook my head at my neighbour, who stepped back one pace, "why do people say bluebird? The bird of happiness isn't blue; the bird of happiness has a pink eyeball, a beak like a spatula, and wings that blush!"

I realized that I had embarrassed my neighbour, who had inquired out of politeness and the expectation of a rote reply. The problem was that Julie's return had jolted me off the surface level at which I'd been living. At this new level, the minutiae of the world pulsed with meaning. Observations at the periphery of my perception skipped effortlessly past my inner censor. At this level, I answered politeness from my depths. I was inappropriate.

The occasional friend, intrigued by eccentricity, laughed and asked how Julie's forearms and fingers had changed.

"Her forearms are muscled, capable, strong, and veined, where formerly they were so unremarkable as to be invisible," I replied. "Her fingers look exquisitely sensitive, as if she had spent fifteen months reading Braille, learning to know a new world through her finger tips."

"And what is the reason for that?"

"I'm not sure. I think it may be the way her physical body is manifesting an inner change."

I talked like that when Julie first got home. Talked in a way that made people squirm a little with the embarrassment I was too intense to feel.

⁂

While Julie was in Japan, I'd written her a letter:

Dear Julie,

This winter I've been fascinated by the idea of the daimon.

"Now what is that?" you're saying.

Well might you ask!

Your daimon is your calling. It's the truest, most essential part of you. It's what you are on this earth to do. Your reason for being. It's your fate, your destiny. Some people say the daimon is the source of creative expression; some say it is a divine power that reveals itself through action.

The Roseate Spoonbill of Happiness

"Now don't get carried away, Mother." I can hear you saying that, Julie, all the way from Japan.

Okay, I won't get carried away, but I have a little story to tell.

When I was a young woman of twenty-five, the age you will be in one month, I had a job at a library. I was the children's librarian. Every week, a little boy of seven or eight would come in. He had brown hair and brown eyes, and he would always take home an armful of books and would talk to us about them when he brought them back. He was our favourite person. His name was David Gregory.

Two years later, when I was twenty-seven, I had a baby girl named Julie. Julie was a lively little girl. At the age of one, she would climb on the sofa and chairs and remove all the pictures from the walls. At the age of two, she would run away down the street if you let go of her hand for one second.

One day, when you were eight years old, I heard you laughing, Julie. I climbed the stairs to see what was so funny.

You were sitting on your bed with the bedroom door open. A Beethoven piano concerto was playing.

"Oh, Mom, just listen to this," you said. You rewound the tape and played a line of Beethoven. You laughed and laughed. You lay back on your bed and guffawed.

I shook my head, puzzled.

"Mom, don't you hear it? It's so funny. Listen." Again you rewound the tape and again you played the line. Your face was roseate with happiness and wet with laughter.

I couldn't hear what you heard. To me it was just a line of Beethoven.

It was then I realized that you were in a special relationship to music.

When you were twelve, you came to me and said you wanted to take flute lessons. I asked your piano teacher to recommend someone.

We went for our first lesson to a house in the west end of the city and knocked on the front door. It opened, and there stood my favourite child from the library, wearing a moustache. David Gregory. Fifteen years older, but the same merry brown eyes and bright smile.

Doesn't that sound like the workings of fate?

13

Since that day, David has been your teacher and mentor and your unfailing supporter. Now he is going to Matsumoto for your graduation recital. What a guy!

Some people have a complicated, troubled relationship with their daimon. Some turn their backs on their daimons for many years. Others let their whole lifetime go by without heeding the call. Your daimon spoke to you when you were very young, Julie. You responded with ardour. You followed your daimon's strict regime: you practiced and practiced.

Last year the daimon called you to go on a long journey. You flew across Canada, across the Pacific Ocean, to Tokyo, Japan. You took a train to the mountains of the north and finally you arrived at the source. Matsumoto. The home of the Suzuki Music School.

You found yourself in a land where you couldn't read the signs or the food packages or the newspaper; couldn't write, couldn't understand what anyone was saying, couldn't ask for directions. In January, when you came home at night to your tiny apartment, the temperature was below zero. When you awoke in the morning, you could see your breath in the air. When you wanted a bath or a shower, you rode your bicycle across town to the gym. You had no phone.

In February, at the age of ninety-nine, Dr. Suzuki died. You took part in the ceremonies surrounding his death. You played your flute in the presence of his body.

Julie, soon you will be coming home. But what you have experienced there, at the source, will stay with you all your life. Through you, the language of music will enter the lives of others, bringing them the kind of happiness you know well.

We are so proud of you, Julie. We send you our love and our very best wishes for the future on this, your special day, the day of your graduation in Matsumoto, Japan.

❧

The first year Julie was in Japan, I did not miss her, or at least was not aware of missing her. I shrugged a cliché at anyone who inquired or empathized: out of sight, out of mind. I'm the mother of an only child now, I would add, blithely.

The "only child" who remained, Emily, felt her status keenly.

She told me that I was just like the mother in the movie, *Secrets and Lies*.

I had seen that movie. The mother was snoopingly intrusive, intensely identified with her daughter, critical, hysterical, unsure where she left off and her daughter began. Even Julie winced when her sister made the comparison, during one of our ten minute, twenty dollar, telephone conversations between Canada and Japan.

"Oh, Emily," she said. The wince was in her tone.

"Emily has put her finger on something, though," I put in, from the extension phone. "I have to admit that I felt a tiny worm of recognition twist in my own gut as I watched that mother. Not that I wanted to. But there was something about the quality of her interest in her daughter's life . . ."

Julie had planned to stay in Japan a year. When she telephoned eleven months into her stay, I asked the question I'd been delaying for fear of the answer.

"When are you coming home?"

The silence on the line told me she wasn't.

She was going to Australia for two weeks. Then three more months in Japan. She'd be home at the end of June.

She'll be changed, people told me. You can't spend fifteen months in a culture so different and not come back changed.

The extra three months of Julie's stay in Japan turned out to be as long as the entire first year of her absence. Once her return was certain, it seemed impossible to wait.

She was scheduled to arrive at the Toronto airport at 10:25 p.m. on the last Sunday in June, after a two hour stop in Atlanta, Georgia. Saturday afternoon, I found myself wandering the long aisles of a box-like store called Parties Plus. The store was part of a new plaza of huge stores reachable only by driving a busy expressway. It was the sort of place I usually avoided. That I was here came under the heading, "Getting Ready For Julie's Homecoming."

"The Party" had become an industry, I realized, as I wandered the aisles. A made-to-order project. You didn't have a party any more; you didn't throw a party; you went to Parties Plus and bought one. Loot bags, loot bag stuffers, hats, candies, streamers, house decorations, cake decorations, prizes, invitations, elaborate candles –

you'd need to work full-time just to pay for your daughters' birthday parties. And everybody's party would look like everybody else's party.

I'd told everyone I was going to make a sign that said, Welcome Home Julie, and tie it to the hedge. I was going to get helium balloons. That's why I was here.

My first attempt at making the sign had failed. The only black magic marker in the house had a fine point. You could barely read the "Welcome Home" at arm's length. I enlarged the letters and tried to colour them in. Colouring in the "W" with the finely-pointed marker took me fifteen minutes and used up the whole thing. I decided to buy a thick marker when I got the helium balloons.

All the markers in Parties Plus were packaged in brightly-coloured cardboard that was encased in a see-through substance that looked like plastic and was impossible to poke through even with my long, sharp fingernails.

"May I help you?" A young, red-haired employee of Parties Plus was gazing at me sadly through his rimless glasses. He had caught me gnawing a package.

"I have to know whether this marker has a fine or a thick point," I told him.

"What kind of a point are you looking for?"

"A thick one."

"That's the kind of point it has."

I didn't believe him. I thought he'd have said it was thin if I'd said I wanted a thin point. There was no way I could make this pale boy understand that Julie would safely cross the Pacific Ocean and the North American continent only if I found the right magic marker and completed my sign.

"I'll think about it," I said, turning my back on him. The sunless aisle of Parties Plus stretched before me, a dreary cake-walk to nowhere. I bought three helium balloons that said Welcome Home, and got out of there.

Next door was a Business Depot. There I found a pair of unpackaged scissors. I used them to cut open three types of packaged magic marker. The third type of marker had a thick point. I bought it.

Back in the car, I didn't think to tether the balloons. They bumped and bobbled about the car as I drove the expressway, inter-mittently blocking the rear view mirror and the back window, making the short trip home from Parties Plus nearly as perilous as I'd imag-ined Julie's twenty-six hour journey to be.

Julie's father would have no part in the making of the sign, the pur-chase of the balloons, the mounting of both on hedge.

"It's going to rain," said Gord, on Sunday morning, when I headed for the back door with the balloons and sign.

"The sun is shining," I pointed out.

"The forecast said occasional showers."

"If it rains, I'll take them down and put them up again when it stops. It's no big deal."

"She won't be here for thirteen hours yet. Why don't you wait till tonight to put them up?"

"Don't even say the word thirteen in the same sentence as Julie," I said. "And do we wait until Christmas morning to put up the tree?"

"Is it the coming of Christ we're celebrating, then?"

I let the screen door slam on my way out, pretending not to hear Gord's rejoinder.

Bachelard said that objects of happiness are always round, that hap-piness rounds out everything it enters. That's why I had to have helium balloons, I guess. In our family, happiness is not only round, it has a fizz to it, and it blushes. It rushes red up the neck and suf-fuses the face and ears. In my father, my sister, me, my two girls – that's how happiness shows itself. And happiness is improbable, somehow – like a pink eyeball at the end of a spatula beak.

When I finally got the sign and the balloons up, I washed the car and vacuumed it. Made Julie's favourite lasagna and put it in the fridge. Weeded the garden, washed my hair, made dinner, ate dinner.

It was still only six p.m. This day was going to be as long as the three months that had seemed as long as the entire year of Julie's absence. That got me thinking about time.

I went into the living room where Gord was reading the paper. "The way I figure it, time is standing still for Julie the whole time she's flying from Tokyo to Atlanta."

"She's so eager to get home, you mean?"

"No, I mean that when she leaves Tokyo, it's five in the after-noon, their time. She flies for thirteen hours and when she lands in Atlanta, it's five in the afternoon – our time. She never adjusts her watch. For the whole thirteen hour flight, time stands still."

"Okay, and . . .?"

"It's hard for me to get my mind around, that's all. That if you go east fast enough, time stands still. That if you go east even faster, time goes backwards. Does that mean that if you spent your whole life going east even faster, you'd keep getting younger? You'd never get old and die?" I walked up to Gord and made googly eyes at him over his newspaper. "Have I, in my preparations for Julie's return, unwittingly discovered the secret of eternal youth?"

"Lizzy, I suggest you try it out. Run over to the park and go east-even-faster. By the time you've finished, you might be twelve years old again. It might even be time to leave for the airport."

On the expressway were many cars. I waited for Gord to ask where all these people were going at this hour of the night.

"Where are all these people going at this hour of the night?"

"Where are you going, Gord?"

"I'm going somewhere unusual. Normally I'd be at home at ten o'clock Sunday evening."

"These people are going somewhere unusual or somewhere usual. They're going home from visiting family or they're on vaca-tion or they're doing an errand that involves highway travel. Like us, some of them may be going to the airport."

"Yeah, Dad," said the only child in the back seat, she whose loss of status was imminent and fervently desired.

There's a condemnatory tone to Gord's oft-repeated remark that troubles me. As if only we are legitimate. The rest are somewhere they shouldn't be. Behind his comment lies a world view: we are the centre of the world; others exist only in that they inconvenience us.

I would hold onto this opinion until the moment we arrived home.

At the airport, we found the glass wall behind which Julie would appear. Gord and I pressed up against it; Emily found a place on the floor some distance away. She leaned her back against a pillar and pretended to read her magazine.

We waited. Many travellers came up the stairs behind the glass wall. At last came a traveller with dark, glossy hair, a blue knapsack, and a smile as wide as a continent.

A startling, salty flood overwhelmed my face and a rush of red suffused my neck and cheeks. I blew my nose and turned to look for Emily in the crowd. "She's here, Emily," I shouted. "Julie's home."

The faces in the crowd looked at me with benign understanding. "Ah, mothers will be mothers, as boys will be boys!" said their eyes. Only one pair of eyes did not. On Emily's face was a look that would quell a geyser. I stopped spouting and beckoned to her. She looked away, pretended not to know me. I turned back to the glass.

It had been fifteen months since I had looked into the face of the radiant young woman who was climbing towards me. In preparation for her homecoming, I had cleaned and weeded and baked and cooked, as women have done through the ages. I had engaged in petty crime and entrusted my life to three helium balloons. I had discovered the secret of eternal youth.

And here she was. Changed in her forearms and her fingers, changed in ways that would be revealed only by the sounds that came from her flute. Yet unmistakably Julie.

As she came through the gate, there was a rush of wings, a strange music that was part cry and part singing. It was the roseate spoonbill of happiness.

As we turned into the driveway, Julie saw the sign. "Oh my God, so the whole street knows I'm home!"

"Your mother is an exhibitionist," said Gord.

Julie opened the car door. Gazelle-leaping out of the darkness and into her arms came her best friend, Laura. The squeals, the tears, the laughter increased my desire for fanfare. Bells should be ringing. I looked around the dark street; I hoped we were making enough noise to waken the dead. At the least, I wanted neighbours in nightcaps out on porches, banging pots and pans.

That night, I was just like Gord. I thought we were at the centre of the world.

Fernando's Life and Our Lives

was afraid of one of my husband's friends. Fernando was his name.

A pregnant friend of mine, Jilly Simpson, was living in our basement that summer. I was pregnant, too. Fernando's wife was pregnant. We were all in the same childbirth class. It was 1965.

Fernando's hair was to his waist, as orange as the fire Prometheus stole from the Gods. His moustache spread everywhere – up his nose, towards his ears, over his top lip. He had orange hair on his neck and in his ears and covering his back. Fernando's pale eyes were like the blue flame of a gas burner and they fastened to your own and burned all the time he was talking.

Ferno was a proselytizing vegetarian. I learned that word in connection with a preacher. As soon as I heard it, I knew it belonged to Fernando. Put it in front of vegetarian and you have quite a title: Fernando Pereira, P. V.

I wasn't afraid Fernando would harm me physically. Nothing like that. Ferno was a draft dodger. In those days, you couldn't go around a Canadian block without falling over a draft dodger. They all had long, easy hair and blue eyes the colour of a baby's bonnet.

They believed it was wrong to kill humans, even in war, but their government was trying to send them to Vietnam to do just that. So up they came to Canada.

Fernando was from Pennsylvania. He didn't believe in killing humans or animals, either. Claimed he could hear the shriek of a carrot when it was yanked from the ground. I was afraid of him because of the way he acted when he saw somebody eating meat.

It was a second baby for all of us. The first time, none of us went to class. Why would we? We were hippies back then. We believed that anything that was part of nature, was, well . . . natural. A person didn't need to go to school to have a baby. In the old days, women squatted in the field to let their babies plop out; they bit off the cord, tied the baby to their backs, and kept on ploughing the field. We laughed at people who went to childbirth class. I went to the hospital when I had laboured for a day with moderate pain. My face was serene as an egg; I expected to have my first child within the hour.

Fourteen hours later, I hollered: "I don't care what you do; I don't care if you kill it, just get it out of me." I made the "me" like a siren – meeeeeeee. The doctor cut me from one hole to the other, entered me with the high forceps, braced his foot on the delivery table, and pulled. There was a glopping, sucking sensation, as if my insides were being yanked out. Along with them came a baby girl we called Kitty. It was two weeks before I could even walk.

My friend Jilly's first baby was born with the cord around his neck. He lived two days. Fernando's wife, Wanda, had as hard a labour as mine.

This time, we went to class. By now we'd noticed that Mother Nature laid on floods and earthquakes and tornadoes as casually as we pulled on our blue jeans. We'd cut our hair and modified our views. Not Fernando, though.

Fernando believed that it was a sin to eat meat. By now, I've come around to seeing things mostly his way. But back then, I was scared of him. I thought he was loony tunes.

I was brought up in a world where you found the trinity on your plate every night: mashed potato, cooked peas, a piece of meat. At the tip of your knife was a full glass of homogenized milk. On your bread and butter plate was a piece of white Wonder bread.

Meat had nothing to do with animals. Meat was what your father went to work to provide. It was the essential building block of your body, the lynchpin of Canada's food rules, the sun of your supper, the apogee of your day. A vegetarian was someone who sat down each night to boiled potato, a heap of pallid lettuce and a great expanse of bare shining plate.

I repeat, I thought Fernando was nuts.

My husband, Tom, taught with Fernando at the Free School. Across the road was a Mom and Pop restaurant where some of the teachers and students ate lunch. Tom would come home and tell me about it.

"Ferno made a scene at Wartley's again today, Lou."

"What'd he do?"

"Bubsy Schultz had three hamburgers with the works. He had them stacked on his plate along with fries and a milkshake."

"And?"

"Ferno walked over to his table and started in. 'The animal whose dead body you're eating ended his days shit-scared in an abattoir that stank like fish guts and skunk. His last sight was the life blood of his fellow critters spouting like the geysers of Hell.'" Tom was bent over, his pointer finger stabbing and shaking. He sounded just like Fernando.

I clapped my hands to my head. "Lordy! What did Bubsy do?" Bubsy Schultz was a huge, bent guy who ducked his head and blushed if you spoke to him about the weather. He cleaned Free School in the morning, then went off to work the afternoon shift at a meat packing plant.

"Turned red and ate those hamburgers in two bites each. Left his fries, took his milkshake, and got out of there."

"He'll probably never go in to Wartley's again. What did Fernando do?"

"Went back to his grilled cheese sandwiches. You know how he has those tics? There were three of them dancing the St. Vitus rag in his face while he ate."

I shook my head. "What if Ferno stops in here some time when we're having meat?"

Tom shrugged. "So what? That's his problem, Louisa. Let him carry on all he wants."

I knew I couldn't. In those days I was the kind of person who was always on guard to know what other people thought. Nod was my middle name. I could make myself agree with a Holy Roller or a Jezebel. I was so tuned in to the unseen currents that flow when people are together in a room that sometimes I didn't even register the content of a conversation.

We didn't lie to Fernando and tell him we were vegetarians. But we knew he assumed we were, and we didn't tell him we weren't. I was so afraid Fernando would come along and catch us eating meat that I kept the doors locked, even in the summertime. Then one day we had company, and Ferno was the last thing on my mind.

Jilly Simpson looked about sixteen. She was a natural-born blond with fair eyebrows, fair eyelashes and a face like the angel that welcomes folks to Heaven on religious Christmas cards. Unlike me. I looked like the deuce half the time. I couldn't be bothered fixing up. When you have a gherkin pickle nose like mine, what's the point?

Jilly was living in our basement because she had to give birth in a high tech hospital, after what happened the first time. Her home was up north in a small town where her husband Jean Luc had a farm instrument dealership. Goderich, Ontario. I come from there, too. Jilly and I knew each other before we came down to London to go to Fanshawe College. Both of us trained to be nurses but both of us got pregnant before we even finished school.

When Jilly went into labour, I phoned Goderich to hunt down Jean Luc, and Tom took Jilly to the hospital. The clerk in Admitting quizzed them.

"Name, Madam?"

"Jilly Simpson."

"And this is Mr. Simpson? Will he be staying with you in the labour room?"

"He'll be staying with me, but Simpson is my name only. My husband's name is Bonenfant."

"Fine, you can sign here, Mr. Bonenfant."

"No, this is Mr. Cauley."

"I thought you said your husband's name was Bonenfant."

"It is, but this isn't my husband."

This was in the days before every other woman was with somebody who wasn't her husband. Back then it was considered daring to have husbands in the labour room.

"Could I ask what relationship Mr. Cauley is to you, if you expect me to allow him in with you?" said the clerk, looking as if she had a poker up her arse. (This is how Tom told it later.)

Jilly said, "He's a friend," at the same time as Tom said, "I'm a surrogate husband." They looked at each other and laughed. They repeated themselves, again in unison. This time, Jilly's laugh turned into a long groan. Admitting waved them on in disgust, I gather.

Tom sat with Jilly, timed her pains, and breathed with her through the contractions. Jean Luc got there in time for the pushing, which produced seven pounds and one ounce of bellyaching baby girl.

Tom and Jean Luc came home as proud as if they'd had her themselves.

I'm getting to where we had company and I forgot about the existence of Fernando Pereira, P. V.

Two days after Jilly had Angie, I had Bunny. Tom took me to the hospital. We got the same admitting clerk.

"This one's my wife," said Tom. "Louisa. She's in labour, too."

"Tell me another one, Sonny," said the clerk, buzzing Security. She was a big woman with white hair and a face like a potato that's been too long in the drawer and is sprouting warts and suchlike.

"No, really, the, uh, woman I brought here the night before last wasn't my wife," said Tom. He scratched his crotch. He looked so guilty even I had trouble believing him.

"Would you send Security down here," said the clerk into the phone. "We got a joker shows up every other night with a wife in labour."

"Would you let meeeeeeeee in at least?" I said. "Or I'm going to have this baby right in Admitting."

That's how I got to deliver Bunny without any help from Tom. Upstairs, my water broke with such force it hit the far wall and ran down in streamlets. The intern ducked. Ten minutes later, Bunny slid into the world. She came so easily I could have bitten off the cord and gone back to ploughing a field.

I was home two days later, in time to confirm with Jilly that the only way to get shit off a cloth diaper was man-u-a-lly – that is wo-man-u-a-lly.

Jilly stayed with us for two weeks. Jean Luc went back up north, but Jilly didn't want to risk going so far from High Tech and her obstetrician until she felt confident that her new daughter was here to stay. I was confident of that from the first day. A screamer like Angela Bonenfant obviously had a hold on life that was in no way tenuous. (Angie's a rising opera diva now. If only we'd known then that all that bawling was in the service of Art!)

Tom was kept busy. Luckily it was summer, and Free School was out. Jilly and I sent Tom to the store for pads to suffocate leaking breasts, for cloth diapers, for disposable diapers, for nipples for the bottles we might need if we didn't have enough milk of our own, for a darning needle to enlarge the holes of the nipples for the bottles we might need, vitamin E oil for sore cracking nipples (ours), a soother for Angela, a soother for Bunny, a soother for Kitty (who had to have everything Bunny had), safety pins with safety heads, diaper rash ointment, ivory snow, baby oil.

Each of these was a separate trip. "Why don't you make me a list with everything on it so I can get it all at once?" Tom said finally. He looked beat. His pony tail looked as if it belonged between a dog's legs.

"We don't know what we need till we need it," we told him, our four blue eyes raised wide to his.

As usual, we were side by side on the chesterfield nursing Ange and Bunny, melon boobs lolling on pumpkin stomachs. We had given birth, we had done what nature put us on earth to do, and now Jilly and I had become one – one mindless, dumb, nurturing animal. We overflowed with milk and a stupid, mute acceptance of the moment. We could no more make a list than we could stop squealing "Ouch!" whenever a set of merciless gums latched on for another feed.

"Never mind, never mind, never mind," said Tom. "What can I do for you now?"

"What's going on with you, anyway?" I said. Usually I couldn't get him to wipe his own arse, and here he was offering to run his twenty-fifth errand of the day. "Feed her," I said, nodding at Kitty, who was sitting beside me, red corduroy legs straight out in front, a doll worrying at her flat, tan disc.

"Nooooooooo," shrieked Kitty, when Tom tried to lead her away. "I noos too." She stiffened her red legs and her face turned cranberry. Tom backed off.

In ten days, Angela went from seven pounds one ounce to eight pounds fifteen ounces, and Jilly began to believe she was here for the duration.

The point is that we bonded. When Jean Luc came at the end of the second week to take Jilly and Angie away, we cried. All of us. Jilly and I cried because we'd been one and now we had to split apart, which left each of us with one side raw and exposed to every blast from life. Tom cried because he was exhausted. Angela cried because that's what she always did. Bunny cried because Kitty was clawing her. Jean Luc cried because Jilly was paying no attention to him, only to Angela.

I made that up. Jean Luc did not cry. He loaded his sobbing wife, his bawling daughter, and several laundry baskets of newly acquired paraphernalia into his pickup truck, and drove away. He had the look of a man who picks up his spade to dig a posthole and finds himself in China.

We had bonded. And so Jilly and Jean Luc and Angela came back for visits. Regular visits. I was so happy to see them that I lost my vigilance. I served black forest ham for lunch and left the outside door open and the screen door unlocked.

I was explaining to Jean Luc my theory of child rearing. Follow the child's rhythm, the way elephants do, I told him. When a baby elephant wants to sleep, he lies down, right there, and the rest of the tribe lies down too and waits for him to wake up.

Jean Luc kept his eyes on my face as I talked. His eyes were glass green and a little too close together, and he had a spiffy, little red moustache. "Follow a child's rhythm for the first three years and you have a secure human being for life," I stated.

"Louisa, you have become a proselytizing parent," said Jean Luc. I had talked about Fernando so much that we all knew that word.

That was all it took. Did you ever notice how true that "Speak of the Devil" thing is? There came a rap at the front door. Tom got up to answer. My wine-loosened tongue was still clickety-clacketing about elephant babies when I heard Ferno's voice. I snapped to in a hurry, I tell you.

Jean Luc had a forkful of pink, black forest ham halfway to his mouth. There was no time for niceties. I snatched that ham right off his fork. The look on his face will stay with me forever. With my other hand, I cleared my plate of ham, as well as Jilly's plate, Tom's plate, and the white platter in the middle of the table. Ham in hand, I ran for the kitchen just as Kitty tootled into the dining room grasping a slew of jujubes and her new recorder. We collided. I left her on her back, howling and choking. (There are times when "follow their rhythm" has to be set aside.)

I threw the ham into the fridge freezer while hollering, "Somebody do the Heimlich maneuver on Kitty." I slammed the freezer door shut and twirled to greet Fernando, who was by now standing in the kitchen doorway with Tom.

"What's going on?" he said. The tic beneath his eye was throbbing like a heart that can't find its way back to its chamber. "Does this commotion have something to do with me, Lou?"

"Not at all," I said, noting with horror that Bunny in her high chair was hamfisted. "Do the Heimlich maneuver," I yelled again at the zombies in the dining room. Kitty was the colour of water when you've steamed purple cabbage and green beans above it: a deep morgue blue.

"What can we do for you, Ferno?" I said, as hostessy as I could manage. "We were just having lunch with Jilly and Jean Luc here. Could I offer you some wine?"

By now, Kitty's eyes were bugging out, so I nipped into the dining room, grabbed her from behind, stood her upright, stuck my fist in her craw and powed her one. They taught me that much at Fanshawe. A wad of purple jujubes shot from her mouth and past Jean Luc's ear just the way my waters sprayed past the intern's face.

Fernando's nostrils were quivering like a slavering dog's. They led him straight to Bunny's fist. As if charmed, she opened her chubby hand to reveal its contents, now pinkly flaccid and trailing drool. Fernando gazed at her, then slowly turned to look at meeeeeeeee.

"Meat," he said, in a tone that made Kitty stop crying and turn around for the show. "Meat In This House." He gave each word an equal thump.

He stepped closer to me. The tic between his mouth and his nose jitterbugged happily.

"Pig," he said. "Dead Pig."

Fernando's breath smelled of sulfur, and up close each of the thousand hairs on his body seemed a potential flame. He turned so he could see all of us, Jean Luc with fork still half-raised; Jilly, her white hair in pigtails tied with pink wool; Kitty, her streamers of snot bubbling with interest; Tom, leaning against the wall looking indulgent; and of course, good old meeeeeeeee, worst nightmare unfolding before her eyes.

"Do You Know," said Fernando, in the tone of a preacher calling sinners to the river, "that piglets kept in factory farms have their tails amputated to prevent tail biting and cannibalism? That sows are housed indoors on concrete slats without bedding? That for years these mother pigs are chained to the ground where they cannot even turn around?" And here Fernando, tics blipping, turned his intensity full on me, "that incarcerated sows undergo birth difficulties that make your fourteen hour labour and queen-sized episiotomy look like a picnic?"

"Do you know," he turned again to encompass us all, "that hog confinement operations are so disease-making that farm workers, who spend but a fraction of their time in the overstocked and so-called environmentally controlled buildings, can suffer acute and potentially serious respiratory problems?"

Tom snapped out of his slump. "I do know that, all of that, yes, I do, Ferno," he said, briskly, "I know it because you've told me. Many times. Yet still I eat meat."

"What is your excuse, Tom?"

"I like meat, Ferno. I enjoy it."

"You don't care about the suffering of animals?"

"I do care, if it's there, in front of me. I hate the whole idea of factory farms. But I guess I choose not to think about it most of the time, not to connect it to the ham on my plate. Just like a million other evils in this old world, Ferno. You could drive yourself crazy if you took all of 'em on."

"To choose not to connect the suffering of animals to what you put into your mouth is an act of moral turpitude."

"Yes, I'd agree with you there too, Ferno. I am morally turpitudinous. I'm a louse."

I was staring at this husband of mine, admiring his gumption. Tom saw the look in my eyes, and he put his arm around Fernando and walked him to the door. "I'll call you, Ferno," he said. "Right now we have guests."

I learned two things that day. One. Hot as Fernando was, he couldn't burn me. Two. My worst fear had happened, and I was still alive. Not only was I alive, I was better off. I didn't have to lock the doors anymore in the summertime.

The story of Fernando Pereira ended last summer, twenty years after he caught us eating meat. Fernando and Wanda split up, and Fernando moved away. The Free School collapsed, Tom got taken on at a high school. We had one more kid. Jilly and Jean Luc moved to Quebec.

I finished my nursing degree at Fanshawe. Eventually we moved back to Goderich where I got a part-time job in a private hospital. I took correspondence courses in psychology, lost some of my piss-and-vinegar, learned about lentil soup and curried rice, gained a little maturity maybe. Subdued. That's the word Jilly used when she visited us last summer. "You're subdued now, Lou, compared to the old days."

Regularly, we'd hear news of Fernando from Wanda. He was in California, working to save the redwoods. He had a new wife. He was in South America, working to save the rainforests. He was divorced again. He was on the Galapagos, documenting the impact of tourism on the ecosystem. He'd moved to Holland, married a Dutch journalist twenty years his junior.

Sometimes, after talking to Wanda, I'd think about Fernando's life and our lives. Four in the morning was my philosophical hour, on night duty at the hospital. I decided Fernando had so much fire in him that he couldn't stay in the daily world most of us live in. He couldn't care about the vibes that go back and forth between people, couldn't even sense their existence; his own fire was making a wind in his ears. He couldn't spend contented time in a backyard, puttering at spring cleanup in the shelter of a sun-warmed wall. His fire was so fierce that it blasted him into the world of Large Causes and kept him there.

I mean, the physical world is so vivid, so sense-drenching real, isn't it! It winds most of us up into its life and makes us forget. We're in a web woven of how the gingerbread house is going to turn out, how the latest software program works, how to choose among buff and sand and terracotta for the kitchen floor. It's so seldom most of us pull free from the seductions of the material world.

Fernando's fire kept him from all that.

The nights were usually quiet on the ward. Sometimes I had CBC Radio on low.

Very early one July morning, the announcer broke in on a program of recorded music: *Authorities have released the name of the crew member who lost his life when the Greenpeace ship, Rainbow Warrior, was sunk off New Zealand yesterday. The man was Fernando Pereira of Holland.*

An hour later, the *Toronto Star* slapped up on the little porch off Reception. I went downstairs and picked it up, found the articles. There was a colour picture of the Rainbow Warrior and one of Fernando Pereira, photographer and Greenpeace crew member. I stared at that page for a long time.

When I got off work at seven that morning, I didn't go straight home. I drove down to the lake, parked the car by the salt mine and walked way out the old cement breakwater.

I half expected a comet, but there wasn't one, of course. A fisherman dangled a silent line above the silver lake. Out there in the misty pink, where water blurs into sky, floated a lost crescent moon.

The invisibly thinning ozone layer, the invisibly acid water, the invisibly warming planet were a presence; the announcer's statement had torn holes in the web I was wound in.

This next is going to sound strange. You're maybe going to think *I'm* loony tunes.

Fernando's hair was the colour of a house sparrow's breast. That's right. His hair was dun-brown. So was his moustache, his ear

31

hair, his back hair, all of his hair. I remembered his hair was brown right after the announcer said his name. For an instant that was almost like a vision; I saw Fernando as he was, literally, back when I knew him. The picture in *The Star* confirmed it.

His hair was brown. Dun-humble. But all these years I'd remembered Fernando Pereira with a nimbus of orange fire, a thousand smaller flames sizzling to life all over his body.

Puck, Puck, P'Gawww

*I*n July, I started leaving my husband jobs. He was off for the summer. I still had to go to work. When I got home at five-thirty, the counters were crumby from breakfast. The kitchen garbage was overflowing and the grass high enough to provide forage for ten cows.

"If you were working and I was home, how would you like to come home and find everything a mess?" I asked Tom. "And no supper?"

Tom didn't say he was a man and I was a woman and that made it different. He just looked as if he was thinking that.

So I started taping a note to the coffee grinder every morning.

"Please move the stove and clean between it and the wall today."

"Please cut back the forsythia today."

"Please take everything out of the basement freezer and wash the insides with baking soda and warm water."

The notes were models of specificity and flat affect – a term I learned at the hospital where I'm a nurse on the Psych ward. The shrinks have their own language. They say "flat affect" when they mean unemotional. The first time I heard a shrink say "flataffect," I thought it was a variation on flatulent. Like, maybe this patient passed gas in a pattern; like Morse code.

The evening of the day I taped up the freezer note, Tom had news for me.

"Guess what, Louisa, I found one of those big, free-range chickens at the bottom of the basement freezer. We got those chickens years ago, when Aunt Bertha was still on the farm."

"Great!" I said, soaping my fingers to remove my rings. "Let's take it with us to the cottage. Put it in the kitchen sink overnight. It can finish thawing in the cat litter pan on the way up north. We'll have roast chicken for dinner on our first evening."

This was a Friday. Saturday, our two-week holiday at the family cottage on Lake Huron would begin. Tom had been getting double notes, even triple notes from me all week.

"Please go to market and buy seven loaves of twelve-grain bread."

"Let loose ten cows onto the lawn and set their mandibles to close-crop."

"Please buy a can of bug spray. I'll bring home a mask from the hospital. Once the rest of us are packed in the car, you can don the mask and go down and spray the basement. By the time we get home from our holiday, the fumes will have dissipated and you'll be able to sweep up a heap of dead silverfish, potato bugs, centipedes, millipedes, spiders, cockroaches-I-hope-not, etcetera. It is not often one's labours are rewarded so tangibly."

The morning after that note, I found a note on the coffee grinder. "Your 'humour' sucks. 'Spray the basement' would be sufficient." I didn't know if the author of the note was Tom, or Kitty, our thirteen year old, but if I had to guess, I'd say Kitty.

The night before we left, I packed, cleaned, and set timers on lamps. I sautéed onions, celery, and mushrooms, broke stale bread into bits, seasoned with sage and savory. Our first dinner at the cottage would be a feast.

"Yummm," said Tom. He can't cook, and I haven't been making regular, home-cooked meals since I went back to nursing when Henny, our youngest, started grade one. Down to the basement he went, hefted that big frozen bird from the freezer, staggered up the stairs and over to the kitchen sink. The chicken landed with a hollow thunk.

"It's huge," I said, poking the icy rump. "Huge. We'll have

chicken all week: chasseur, marengo, tetrazzini, caccciatore!" Tom's face was like a February amaryllis in bloom.

In the morning, I went straight to the kitchen sink.
My hand never reached the tap. There was the plastic bag on its side, empty. Ice in the shape of a finger. No chicken.
I looked around. I even opened the broom closet where I kept the long-handled magic duster made in China that I'd bought recently at the Biway. On the end of the long handle was an efflorescent puff of lime-green, candy floss-pink, and lemon yellow. Now, whenever I talked on the phone to my mother, I walked around the house on tip toe, stretching to dust high ceilings and out-of-the-way corners. It felt wonderful. I was killing four birds with one magic duster from China: talking on the phone, doing housework, doing tai chi, setting Tom a good example.
There was no partly-thawed chicken in the duster closet.
"Mingo!" I exclaimed. The cat looked at me without flinching. Thin, grey, and bulimic as always. Just to be sure, I checked the house for a cat cud of fowl or a pile of bones, and saw only the zooming hind end of several centipedes. I did discover my sleeping husband, a beatific look on his face, obviously dreaming of chicken divan.
Bunny and Henny, our two youngest, were already up north at my sister's. By noon, Tom and Kitty and I had all made a fowl-less search. "This sucks!" said Kitty. She'd just turned thirteen and her vocabulary had suddenly expanded: that sucks, take a downer, she's crusty, he's nasty, yaaaa.
I sat down on the only kitchen stool we had left. The rest were in the basement. "Please glue rungs back on stools" would be my first note when we returned from vacation.
"Maybe somehow it was still alive," I suggested. "I've heard of young children surviving frigid water for hours. A hypometabolic state. Maybe it got away – you know, took up its ice and walked!"
"Sure, Louisa," said Tom. His blue eyes watered, the blond tufts over his ears drooped. "Beheaded, plucked, its guts in a plastic bag, at the bottom of a freezer. Sure." The tone of this remark had a no-dinner-again tinge to it.
"Well then," I said, with one last furtive peek at the ceiling, "I

can only conclude that there never was a chicken. Just a huge hunk of ice."

"And who would carefully wrap a lump of ice the size of a chicken in a plastic Eaton's bag and put it in our freezer beneath the tons of frozen peaches from your fleeting good-little-wife period?" Tom swung around and started up the stairs. "That seems about as likely as the thing being alive."

Phoning my mother and sister to tell them our expected arrival time, I related to them the mystery of the disappeared chicken.

"You haven't cleaned your freezer since I got you those free-range chickens from Aunt Bertha?" interrupted my sister. "You haven't cleaned your freezer in *five years?*"

"Remember, there *is* no chicken," I said. "We don't know that it's five years since your brother-in-law cleaned the freezer, Joanie. There is no chicken."

"You thawed it in the sink? And the trunk? You could have died of salmonella poisoning," screeched my mother.

"Remember, there is no chicken," I said, quite loudly, into the phone.

I had asked the new, young shrink from the hospital to house-sit for us. He was renting half the duplex across the road. I figured regular tasks such as putting our *Globe and Mail* inside and watering our containers of purple petunias would help keep him grounded.

"The basement!" he said, when he came for the key and I told him about the chicken. "Hmmm. The basement would be the unconscious. You and Tom retrieve a great frozen lump from your unconscious." He fingered his crescent nose ring thoughtfully. "By your joint efforts, you bring it to the kitchen, the heart of your home. There it melts, and you see that though it is a corporeal entity, yet it has wings, it can fly . . .

"Martyn," I interrupted, there IS NO CHICKEN."

"What are we going to have for dinner tonight, then?" said Kitty. "Nada, nada, as usuala? What are you going to do with the dressing?"

"Kitty," I said, slapping the butcher knife against the carving knife, "get upstairs and pack, lest I eviscerate and stuff *thee!*" I sprang at her like a fencer. "Your father wouldn't know the difference between that and Cock-a-leekie, anyhow."

When I walked up to the kitchen sink expecting to see a partly-thawed chicken, and saw instead a finger of ice, my heart did a delighted flip, the way it always does when I'm truly surprised. It seemed that a miracle had happened in our stainless steel kitchen sink.

"There is no chicken," I'd said, to my sister, my mother, and our house-sitter. But oh, how I wanted there to have been one!

Some people say it's a miracle when you leave your wallet in a store and it's still there when you go back. But that's not a miracle; it's a statement about the dishonesty in our society. A woman sawed in half and made whole, or a pigeon emerging from a sleeve is not a miracle. It's a trick. It's not a miracle when a doctor pronounces a woman full of cancer and she presents herself cured two years later, not a trace of disease in her body. All that proves is that doctors don't know everything. A miracle isn't a story about a statue of the Virgin Mary over in Italy with tears sliding from her stone eye sockets. There's something going on we don't know about.

I wanted there to have been a frozen chicken in our kitchen sink and I wanted its disappearance to be a miracle. But it was beginning to look as if we'd never know.

We arrived at the cottage mid-afternoon and discovered that the lake had taken back part of the beach. This had been the rainiest summer in years. Tom and I carried our luggage inside, then sat down on the front patio in the sun, the vast blue lake before us. Next door, Betty McIlraith was cutting the grass with a hand mower. An innocent friendly sound. To me, the smell of new cut grass is the smell of summer. It always brings me an image of my dad as he was years ago, pushing the hand mower, his bare arms burnt by the sun, hairs of gold along their reddened, muscled surface.

On the other side Jeff McGrath was showing the cottage he rents by the week. It seemed he was always showing it. This couple looked to be in their sixties and their car had Michigan license plates.

"It's the last week of August we'd be wantin' it fer," the man was saying. "How are you fer bugs in these here parts? We were further north this week, fishin', and the bugs was pretty bad."

"Oh yeah, well, there's bugs alright, sure, but no more'n usual," said Jeff. "Yous've been up here before." With his forearm he wiped sweat from his forehead and temples.

Jeff's five year old son was part of the conversational circle. He had his arms folded across this chest, just like the grownups. He looked up at the man from Michigan and spoke proudly, his high voice carrying clearly over the sound of the little waves. "My Dad says the bugs is so big this year they're fuckin' the chickens."

When the laughter had died down and Jeff McGrath's face had lost its blush, I leaned over to Tom. "Damn, that's the one place I didn't look. In bed with the centipedes."

"Very funny, Louisa. What are *we* having for dinner?"

"I told you, Tommy. Dressing à la dressing."

For me, a miracle is like this:

It's a sultry day in summer and Lake Huron is quiet, the waves light slaps against the stony shore. The occasional gull dipping and crying. I'm on my back on an air mattress, the kind with an extra swelling at one end for your head. I've just washed my hair and wrapped it in a pink towel. Beside me on the mattress is a bottle of shampoo and conditioner, a pink and white striped facecloth, a bar of soap, and a frightened daddy-long-legs. I'm thinking I shouldn't lie in the sun for so long, but it feels good. Then I see a man coming towards me.

The man is clad in a blue towel that's knotted around his waist. He's walking on the surface of the water. I'm straining my neck to see, thinking he must be wearing some device on his feet I haven't heard of yet – seven-fathom-tall flippers or something.

He walks right up to me and stops. His head is shaved except for a strip of blue hair, a crest, like an Iroquois warrior's. There's nothing on his feet.

"Hello," I say.

He nods.

"Who are you?"

"Who do you say that I am?" He says this not sarcastically, but gently and seriously, his blue eyes meeting mine.

"Well, you seem to be walking on water."

He nods. His crest bobs up and down.

"Well, the only person I know of who can walk on water is Jesus Christ."

He nods again. "I am He."

It's my turn to nod. "You must be. No mortal uses the subjective case like that anymore. But I wouldn't expect Jesus to have blue hair gelled into a crest."

"I am eternal, Louisa, but when I take on a temporal form, I present myself in the idiom of the day."

"This *is* a miracle, then, for me to see you right here on Lake Huron. Thanks very much for coming, Jesus."

"You're welcome. You deserve it, Louisa, working so hard all day and coming home to a husband who leaves crumbs on the counter. I'll be going now and I'll take daddy long legs with me. He's frantic. I'll drop him on shore before I evanesce."

"That would be compassionate of you, Jesus. And seeing as you're here, do you do things like grant three wishes, or anything like that?"

Jesus laughs so hard I'm afraid his towel is going to drop off. Oh, okay, I *hope* his towel is about to drop off. Imagine being able to intone, truthfully: "I have looked upon the genitalia of the Lord, and it was good." His laugh makes him shake all over and on his forehead the little marks where the crown of thorns dug into his flesh turn red. "Oh, no, Louisa, I leave that for the fairy godmothers."

Jesus leans over and touches the mattress with his index finger. As he opens his hand, I see the scar on his palm. The spider runs up his arm and neck, over his shaven scalp, and into his blue hair. Jesus walks on the water all the way to the shore, gently shakes the spider from his crest, and disappears.

That's what I mean by a miracle. It has to be like that.

I wanted our disappeared chicken to be a miracle of that order. I wanted this to be a world where I could stand on the shore of Lake Huron and tell my three kids: "Listen girls, out there, way out there where sea turns into sky, there's a big, ice-caked chicken from the depths of an unconscious freezer, flying free."

That evening, Tom and I brought dinner out to the front patio where we sipped wine and ate dressing. It was quiet, Henny and Bunny not due to arrive until the next day. We watched the setting sun trace topaz filigree upon indigo blue.

Tom spooned the last morsel of dressing from the bowl. "Puck, puck, p'gawww!" he cackled.

"Oh, shut up," I said.

Then Kitty appeared before us. "I brought all my old diaries up to this boring place," she announced. "And guess what I just found."

I shrugged and began to clear the table. "No, listen, Mom," she said. "Listen."

She read a page aloud. The page described how she and her friend Selly put a huge plastic bag full of snow at the bottom of our basement freezer, back when they were in grade six.

"You just read that today-right-now?" I said, sitting back down.

"Yeah. Me and Selly did it three years ago. I forgot all about it till I read it here."

"Wow, Kitty, that's amazing. I can hardly believe it! That *that* passage from a journal of three years ago surfaced *today*."

"So," said Tom slowly, looking over at me. "So. There was no chicken."

Just like that, he let go of our miracle.

Stories and The Story

I. Corn

 hate corn.

These words are spoken by her daughter who sits opposite at the supper table. It is September. Later, she will call her daughter to the window to see the harvest moon, a still life pumpkin almost close enough to pick from the sky. Her daughter will say she is finished with coming to the window to see a crusty flock of geese or the moon.

"I hate corn," says her daughter. "I hate the way people's noses spread when they're eating it and the way they have corn hanging from their cheeks when they put down the cob. I hate the sound people's jaws make when they gnaw it and how the corn sticks between their teeth. I hate the way the kernels pop open, like zits. I hate how the cobs feel cold and slobbery when you make me take them to the compost. I hate the broken kernels that are hanging from them. I hate corn."

"Why do I feel it's me you hate, not corn?" she says.

"There you go again." Her daughter jumps up, knocking over her chair. "That's what I mean. You take everything personally. I tell you I hate corn and you say I hate you."

Her daughter mounts the stairs to her bedroom above the kitchen. Fee, Fi, Fo, FUM. She slams what is left of her door. Thirty seconds later, the crackle of Nirvana infiltrates the kitchen ceiling.

The mother looks at her husband, whose place at the table is between wife and daughter. "I am going to tell you a story," she says. "I am going to tell you The story," she corrects herself.

Once upon a time, fifteen years or so ago, the way humans figure it, a woman gave birth to her last child, a daughter. The girl had white gold hair, soft hands, and long fingers. She was a gentle child who brought joy into her parents' lives.

In September, the season of the harvest, the mother called the daughter to her side. This is your fifth year on earth, she said. This fall, you are old enough to help me shuck the corn.

What's shuck? asked the little girl.

To shuck is to strip off the green home of the corn so the part that is good to eat can come out, said the mother.

The child sat beside the mother on the back steps and with her soft hands pulled off the papery green strips, one by one.

Good for you! said the mother.

As the little girl removed the last green strip, a handful of straight, gold, corn silk swung free. The child looked up. On her face was the aha, the expression of all seekers at the moment of illumination.

The corn has blonde hair! she said. Just like me! . . .

II. Nirvana

"Stoners," the word reads. "Stoners." Above the word, a crude drawing of two girls. Staggering, out of their minds. Stoned. Slowly the mother lets herself down on the messy bed.

She looks down at her hand, at the peach. She was about to eat a peach this September afternoon when she glimpsed the papers in the jumble of sheets on the bed she was about to make. Unease had flamed, and her hand reached out to grasp, to read.

She lifts her head. Her eyes move to the window wall, to two posters, side by side. A kitten on its hind legs batting at raindrops, next to the rock group, Nirvana. Stoned. To be stoned out of your mind is cool. Dave, Krist, and Kurt. Three of them, staring at her. Kurt Cobain, dead by his own hand, now a ghost with faint and ghastly radiance wandering the halls of nirvana.

On her daughter's bed, she holds herself and rocks. Back and forth she rocks to Nirvana lullaby. Nirvana. The final beatitude that transcends suffering, karma, and samsara. Nirvana. A place or state of oblivion to care, pain, or external reality. Nirvana. A goal hoped for but apparently unattainable. Nirvana lullaby.

It is only yesterday that she, a girl of fifteen, turned a face of stone towards her own mother who beseeched her to talk, to reveal what was within. It is only a few years ago that she, a woman of forty, at last forgave her own mother for reading her diary.

She looks down at the peach, raises it to her cracked lips. As her teeth break the dry fuzz of the skin, it is as if she is taking a bite out of a small animal. Sitting there on her daughter's bed, she re-enters the story.

Her last child, the baby with the soft hands and the long fingers was born with a tiny cyst in the skin at the hollow of her throat. Nothing to worry about, said the doctor.

When the child was two, the cyst swelled to golf ball size, and the doctors put the child to sleep and removed the cyst with sharp knives. When the wound healed, there was a thick, raised scar, shiny like the nude body of a baby bird.

What is that? said the doctor, when he saw the child again.

I was hoping you could tell me, said the mother.

It turned out the child was one of those rare people whose skin forms a keloid scar whenever it is deeply cut.

The mother taught the child that over the history of humankind, people decorated their bodies with paint, with tattoos, with scars. To remain in a natural state was to be no different from the beasts. The mother showed the child pictures of the scar-decorated legs of the Tivs of Nigeria and the tattoos of the Polynesians. A scar can be either beautiful or ugly, she told the daughter. It depends how you look at it. You.

As the little girl grew, the scar became larger and fleshier and redder. People stared. They questioned. They averted their eyes.

Even when she became a teenager, the girl did not cover the scar with high-buttoned shirts.

I can tell a lot about a person, she said, by how they react to my scar.

I do not have to worry about a daughter like this, thought the mother.

III. The Photograph

A sudden darkness on this autumn afternoon. Flashes illuminate the corners. From above, the hammering of Thor. Then rain, tubs and tubs of it dumped on her roof, on the earth.

She hastens to close the windows. The last room her daughter's. Sill and floor soaked, and the front of her skirt, in the time it takes to lower the window. As she turns away, she sees herself in the white-framed mirror of the dresser.

"Mirror mirror on the wall," she says aloud, leaning towards her reflection, "who is fairest". . . and now she sees the picture, stuck between the mirror and the frame, at eye level . . . "of them all?"

It is a picture of her daughter in a close, head-to-toe embrace with a boy. A young man. The seventeen year old from Poland, guest at her sister's cottage this summer. From across the room, that first evening, she had seen the intense brown eyes follow her daughter as she carried dishes to and from the table.

They are cheek to cheek facing the camera. Her daughter smiling, entranced, blue eyes and blonde hair giving forth light. Around her the boy has both arms pulling her close, his expression serious, intense. Behind and around them, vegetation unnaturally lush, more like the Elysian fields than Muskoka in August.

She stares. This is like coming across her cat, one time, three blocks from home, upside down in a sandbox, a stranger rubbing her belly – her cat – whom she had believed never left her backyard. Now she remembers her daughter's fascination, last spring, with the story by Joyce Carol Oates: "Where are you going, where have you been?" The story of fifteen-year-old Connie, lured away by Arnold Friend, a figure who seems more than man, more than human.

At last, followed by single plunks from the eavestroughs, she tip-toes from her daughter's room.

At lunchtime next day, she returns, steals into the bedroom, takes the picture to the store that does colour copies. Replaces the original as it was, in the mirror.

The next day she walks to the park, sits under a tree and looks at the picture, relives another part of the story.

. . . The child with the soft hands and the white gold hair is the one who still sits in the mother's lap at age eleven, the one who assures the mother she will always sit there. Some part of the mother believes this. The mother let the world take her other children, but this is her baby. In the old tales, the last daughter is the one who stays home, the one who never marries, the one who nurses and comforts the mother in her old age . . .

Back home from the park, wanting to gaze at the photograph again, she looks for it, lifts the notebook in which she stuck it, holds the notebook upside down, shakes it, turns her blue carry-all inside out, finally retraces her steps to the park. Nothing.

What has she done? Her daughter's image lost, left to drift loose in the world.

She starts for home, and her feet beat the sidewalk, "Where are you going, where have you been? Where are you going, where have you been?" She quickens her steps, for the next part of the story must be lived.

. . . Emily Bronte, Jane Austen, Chaim Potok, George Eliot, the mother feeds them through the bedroom door and yes, when she taps to say goodnight – though the tape deck throbs Nirvana – the daughter is reading them, still reading. Though she no longer talks to the mother, no longer seems to listen, the girl-woman is still reading, as she always has, the books the mother feeds her: The Snow Leopard, The Prime of Life, I Know Why the Caged Bird Sings, Lives of Girls and Women; and as the mother searches the shelves for the next one and the next, her heart is no longer confined to her chest; it beats in her bones, in her blood, in her throat, beats with the life of her struggle, her, the mother – Mother – loving and terrible . . .

Strawberry Hill

On the short drive home from work, I see three birds flying, each carrying something bigger than itself: A robin with a kite tail of toilet paper. A sparrow trailing shreds of foolscap. A blue jay with a ruff of cardboard.

It is June third. We've had a cold, rainy spring, and this is the first glorious day. The tree branches are indistinct beneath delicate green lace. Into the open window of the car comes the scent of new mown grass. The privet hedges are white with blossom, the lilacs just over, blue forget-me-nots everywhere in green grass. I enter the house smiling, the bird story on my lips.

You are sitting on the living room couch, staring into space. You have been my husband for twenty-nine years, yet today you look at me as if I were a stranger. I sit down carefully, and wait.

"They phoned this afternoon with my results," you say. "I have breast cancer."

From the valley town of Dundee, a steep, curving road I call Strawberry Hill takes me to the top of the cliff that surrounds the town. Up here, I am suddenly in country, fields unrolling into the distance under an almighty sky. There is a stand that sells fruit and vegetables that come straight from farmers' fields and gardens and orchards. From up here, you can see the world.

On my right as I ascend the steep hill is a small, stone wall. It blocks any view of the steep drop. As the car slowly ascends the hill, I see only sky. Buff and grey stone against blue sky.

Going up, I feel as I'm on the edge of the world.

"If I'm to believe my dreams, something big is about to hit us," I tell you. We are out for our usual evening walk of two miles. It is the rainy, windy first day of June.

"Why, what did you dream?"

"Oh, they've been incredibly vivid the last three nights: an expressway that was being built across our front yard; a tornado that screamed through the house, smashing everything; a cobra on top of a mountain, rearing up and rattling its coils at me."

"Sounds like something's trying to get your attention."

Neither of us connect my dreams to the biopsy results we're expecting in a couple of days. You went to a doctor several years before about the growth on your chest, just above your left nipple. You were told there was nothing to be concerned about. You went back a week ago because the thing appeared to be infected. It was giving off heat.

This doctor sent you for a biopsy.

"I have to have a modified radical mastectomy," you are saying, on the afternoon of June third. "I have to go for tests to see whether it's already spread to the bones or the lungs." You sound as if you are reciting a part in a play. "Katey knows. She came home just as I was on the phone."

"What did she say?"

"Mom will spazz."

"Where is she now?"

"It's Tuesday. She's at work till six."

I am already spazzing. In my own way. My bones are dust, my blood colder than melting snow, my skin running with fire and prickles.

Breast cancer. Even as you say the word, the future unrolls before me. The tests, the waiting, the surgery, the waiting, the chemotherapy, the waiting, the Damoclean sword, the waiting, the first metastases, the waiting, the treatment, the waiting, the slow progression, the waiting, through bones, the waiting, or lungs, the waiting, or brain, the waiting, the deathbed, the waiting, the death, the funeral, the burial, the end.

This was supposed to be my story, not yours. That's how I know it so well. One in nine North American women. I have followed this story in newspapers and magazines. I have watched this story, in colleagues, in friends, in friends of friends, in mothers of friends, in great-aunts. One of every nine.

I will not spazz in front of Katey. Just because she says I will. When she gets home, supper is on the table, as usual.

"The news Dad got today isn't good," I say, "but we don't really know anything yet."

"What do you mean?"

"There are so many different kinds of breast cancer, and they all behave differently. We won't really know anything until they've taken it out and analyzed it. That'll be about six weeks from now. It's quite likely Dad'll be fine, once he has his operation. There's no sense even worrying until we know if there's anything to worry about."

That's my logical, sensible mind talking, not my powdery bones or my melting blood. And it's enough for Katey. She picks up where she left off at dinner last evening, asking her Dad questions about the troubles in Northern Ireland. She has an essay to write.

At the Farmer's Market in our city, you used to be able to get corn picked that morning, peas right off the vine. But over the years, the vendors have lost their association with the farms. Most stalls now display the whole range of vegetables you see at a supermarket.

In June, I visit the Market every day, watching for the strawberries to come in. Some of the stalls have them by the second week. But you can tell from the smell they aren't local. They've been refrigerated and trucked in from the States.

Having discovered one of the few vendors who sells his own produce, I return faithfully. A man and his wife, often sunburned from their labour in the fields. They sell peas and strawberries in June, raspberries in July, corn and peaches in August.

One day, I make small talk with my stall owner. I mention his wife. "That's not my wife," he says. "She just works here."

The next time I walk past, I notice my stall owner talking to the man in the adjacent stall, one that sells everything. The two men look like brothers.

One Monday, my stall has strawberries. I lean over, breathing in their fragrance. There are two scents that for me connote trust. One of these is the scent of a broken tomato vine. The other is a fresh-picked strawberry.

I'm not quite getting it. "Are these from here?" I ask the man.

He looks at me. His eyes in his tanned face are morning glory blue. "I picked them this morning."

I buy two boxes and take them home. The taste is not as I remembered it.

The smell meets me when I come into the kitchen the next morning. The smell of strawberries that are past it. Goodness and trust gone bad. A smell that puts me in mind of butcher shops, slabs of raw meet, blood stains on a white smock.

I have been betrayed by my stall owner. He has sold me berries from the States. He has lied to me. I remember his resemblance to the adjacent vendor. Probably my stall owner is not even a farmer.

That's how I start going to Strawberry Hill.

Tuesday night, I don't sleep. You sleep twelve hours, eat a Father Bear size bowl of porridge for breakfast. I run to the bathroom a dozen times. You sit on the back deck under the trumpet vine reading the newspaper. You have the breast cancer; I do the worrying for both of us.

Later in the week, when I come home from work, I notice a peculiar little place in the garden - stones, blackened twigs lying every which way. I ask you about it.

I had a little fire ceremony last night, you tell me. Like they do at the workshops.

Three times a year, you've been going to the States for week-long workshops training you to become a shaman. A person who enters the other world, at his peril, and brings back a special knowledge to his people. Some people call the shaman the wounded healer.

Where is your wound? I have sometimes wondered that.

After dinner, I ask you to drive Katey and her friend downtown to the movie.

"Ah, oh, I don't know. Maybe you'd better do it."

"But Gene, you always drive them. It's sort of your job, like cooking dinner is mine."

"I, ah, may have had too much wine at dinner to drive."

I look at the bottle of Estrella on the counter. It is empty. You opened it half an hour before dinner. I had one glass.

It comes to me, then. Now, after a few days, you are beginning to think about what is ahead of you. My reactions are always immediate, intense. Yours come more slowly. Why can I never remember this?

"Well, sure, I can take the girls. I need stuff from the pharmacy, anyhow."

You are a man with a woman's disease. That's the aspect of breast cancer that many men find most difficult to deal with, says the material I find on the internet.

It doesn't bother you. In fact, it is the only aspect of having breast cancer that pleases you. That you would have something rare. You have always liked being set apart.

You have always been the outsider.

You return from a day of tests followed by an appointment with the surgeon. I'd wanted to go with you, but you said there was no point. I'd have to leave to go to a meeting in the afternoon, which meant we'd have to take two cars. It would be hard to find a parking space for even one.

"We can park in the underground garage, Gene. We can pay, just for this once." I look into your eyes. I need you to need me in the room as the machine searches your bones.

You shake your head. "There's no point. I'll be fine."

Now you have good news: The surgeon says eighty percent of people survive ten years with the sort of breast cancer your biopsy indicates. That sounds pretty good to you. The best case scenario is a mastectomy followed by hormone pills.

"What's the worst case scenario?"

You laugh an ironic laugh. "He didn't say, and I didn't ask."

I know, of course. I know this story.

And I know that even in the best case scenario, even when there's nothing visible but a scar across your left breast, we'll be living with the sword of Damocles above our heads. The sword that hangs by a single hair.

Your chest was too big for the X-ray machine. You tell me that more than once. Later, I hear you telling Katey.

Strawberry Hill is the only place where I am not worrying, not waiting. The journey is a climb out of the city, out of the world of people. A Jack-in-the-Beanstalk climb from one world to another. Up and up you go in your labouring car, up to the innocent fields and orchards, the fresh fruits and vegetables, the gentian-blue sky and gentle puffs of cloud. There is no fee fi fo fum giant on Strawberry Hill, no sword hanging by one hair. Up here, the wind is always blowing. Up here, the spirit and breath of life is active, invisible, a shaping, creative power whose presence you cannot forget – as you may in the valley, as you may moving along the streets of the city.

A year and a half earlier. December. You and I are on a walk. As we pass the park, heads bent against the cold wind, we are suddenly buffeting one another with intense words.

You are telling me there does not have to be suffering in life. That suffering is in the mind. That one can not suffer.

I disagree. Suffering is part of life, I tell you. Most of us, all of us, unless we are Indian yogis who have spent our lives developing control of our minds and bodies, will suffer intermittently right to the end of our lives.

No, you say. No. It is possible to replace suffering with joy.

"Have you done it?"

"Yes. Yes, I think so."

"What if you get cancer?"

"That's just suffering of the body."

"Huh. Suffering of the body is suffering. Don't dismiss it like that. You don't know what you're saying. Watch out, or fate will teach you what suffering of the body is like. You won't call the suffering of cancer 'just' once you've endured it. You won't say it's only suffering of the body, either."

We walk the rest of the way in silence.

I can't guess your thoughts. Mine are to wonder how you can have reached the age of fifty-seven and hold such a view, a view that calls loudly to life. Life, take me in hand: Life, teach me a thing or two.

The wind is at our backs now. As we head for the opening in our hedge, I glimpse your blue Chev parked in the driveway, and it comes to me why I dislike your bumper sticker: "Say yes to life and love." It's because saying yes to life and love implies saying no to death and suffering. Saying yes to life and love implies turning one's back on the dark side of life. It implies that we human beings can do that.

But we can't. It takes both light and darkness to make the whole. If we cleave determinedly to the light, we will constellate the darkness. We will almost ensure that it comes for us, bearing sharp little teeth and a stomach that growls.

The X-rays, the blood tests, the scans of your bones and your lungs come back clear. There is no visible evidence that the cancer is anywhere but in your breast. After these results, you sleep, eat, read, laugh, and talk as you always have.

You are not spending these perfect days at beauty's zenith waiting, worrying.

I am, though.

Except on Strawberry Hill.

In Ontario in 1997, a modified radical mastectomy is an outpatient procedure.

"How many days will Gene be in the hospital?" people ask me. "One," I tell them. "They'll be releasing him into my hands that same evening."

The common reaction is shock. A "what is our health system coming to?" indignation.

My close friends grin and say, "To you? They're releasing him to *you?* Father forgive them, for they know not what they do." I feign indignation, but I know the sort of thing they're referring to. One Boxing Day evening, tucked into the bottom shelf of her bathroom cupboard, my sister discovered a plate loaded with Christmas dinner – turkey, dressing, mashed potatoes, the lot. She brought the plate into the living room, explained where she'd found it. All eyes turned as one to me.

As it happened, I had not absent-mindedly misplaced my

Christmas dinner, but even I knew it would have been in character.

In the room chosen as sickroom, I change the sheets, wash the floor, damp wash the furniture, dust the corners, windex the windows, sweep the ceiling, replace a burnt out bulb, ready the garbage, place a tray with Kleenex, empty glass, and straw beside the bed. The day before your surgery, I pick a single red rose and put it on the desk in a blue vase. I dredge my psyche for the nurse who must lurk somewhere therein.

I am ready.

Your preparations are different. The morning of the operation, I am awakened at six forty-five by a tapping in the eavestroughs. A scrabbling, persistent, bird-claw sound. I get up, go downstairs and outside.

You have hauled out the high ladder, you have mounted it, and you are cleaning out the eavestroughs. On an empty stomach, before seven in the morning.

You have never been a handyman. You have never been one to rise early. You get vertigo on a ladder. Cleaning out the eavestroughs has been a job you might get to one year in five – at dusk, the light fading fast, me nagging and holding the ladder.

"What on earth are you doing, Gene?"

"I'm getting ready for the operation,"

"Oh, I see. Yes, of course."

The strawberries from the stand on Strawberry Hill are fresh-picked that very day. They are a deep, sweet red, luscious and intense. If ecstasy has a taste, this is it.

For the three weeks of every year that strawberries are in season, they are all I eat. They are my breakfast, lunch, dinner, and bedtime snack. I make a biscuit, top it with strawberries, top that with vanilla yogurt.

Eating berry meals four times a day for three weeks does not diminish for me the intense pleasure of the taste of the strawberries. Every year, I revel in my last meal of berries as much as in my first.

Gene and Katey dislike my passion for strawberries. They tire of The Meal after a couple of days. They crave other food. Usually, I let them fend for themselves during these three weeks. This year, in a concession to breast cancer, I make dinner for them, regular dinners – spaghetti, pasta, salmon loaf, pizza. We sit at the table together. They eat their dinner, I eat mine. Occasionally I say, Mmmmmmm. They twirl spaghetti on their forks and roll their eyes.

In this country we retain a few resounding titles from days of yore: The Victorian Order of Nurses. The Imperial Order of the Daughters of the Empire.

After the mastectomy, the VON come every morning. Fat, thin, young, old, uniformed, not uniformed, the VON are like snowflakes or fingerprints. We never see the same one twice. That is how it becomes possible for me to dupe them.

The first time is unintentional. That day, I am in the living room with you when the VON steps inside. "Gene?" she says, looking at her paper, then looking at you. "Gena?" she says, looking at her paper again, then looking at me.

"Gene," I say. "Greater love hath no man than this, that a man have breast cancer for his wife." The VON frowns. You laugh.

The second time is deliberate.

Two plastic tubes exit from your chest, draining into a plastic bottle. A week post-op, you are sick of the tubes. Your flesh around the entry points is an angry red, wanting to reject the foreign object so it can close and heal. Your flesh is itchy. The necessity to wear the tubes and bottle means that one of your arms cannot enter the sleeve of your shirt. The tubes and bottle disturb your sleep.

The VON's refuse to remove the tubes until "less than twenty-five c.c.'s of sanguinous discharge" drain over twenty-four hours, even though you've had the benefit of the drainage for a week now, even though the old way was not to have tubes at all, just to put up with the swelling. On your eighth day post-op, I carefully falsify the records so that they add up to twenty-five c.c.'s of fluid.

The VON is troubled, suspicious. A very sudden drop, she says, looking from you to me. I look directly into her eyes, as the stall owner looked into mine. "I am positive our figures are correct," I state. "The fluid tapered right off."

She phones her supervisor. They confer. She returns to the bedroom and pulls the tubes. When she's gone, you shower, you dress in jeans and a shirt. You look normal.

While you make a brief foray to the wine store, I phone my mother to boast.

"You deceived the VON?" she says. "How could you? They know best." My mother is old and frail. She is genuinely shocked.

Suddenly my glee, my phoning to tell my mother this news, seems childish. She's been right all those times she said I had "a piece of the old Nick" in me.

At two weeks post-op, my stomach is knotted, my hands cold. We have waited long enough for the pathology report, I suggest. Yes, you say, you are ready to know. But both our family doctor and your surgeon are on holiday.

I call the back-up surgeon's secretary and explain the situation. She agrees to ask whether Dr. Kiss can phone the hospital and get the pathology report for us.

They might call you, I tell you, as I leave for work. Don't call me, because then, if I don't hear from you, I'll think it's bad.

At ten after four, I walk in the back door. You are in the kitchen. You come towards me and I see in your eyes and your shoulders that you know. Whatever it is, you possess it. That is all I can tell as you walk towards me. The time it takes for you to cross the kitchen is, for me, like the instant when an accident is inevitable but not-yet. Into that instant springs clear-seeing and a life.

"The lymph nodes are clear," you say. I fall against you and we hug. Our eyes are wet. They are streaming. We step apart, then hug again, a hug with the strength of the wall at the edge of the world.

"There's more," you say. "It's probably not what the biopsy said, probably not a true breast cancer. It's a rare kind of tumour that probably just happened to be on the breast. It's almost certainly local. Dr. Love says it's a much better diagnosis than breast cancer."

So. Not even the Damoclean sword.

"Dr. Kiss," I say. "Not Dr. Love." I hug you again, blow my nose. "But the mistake is understandable."

That evening I go to Strawberry Hill.

As I go up, the edge of the world seems a familiar place.

The sky is lavender. There is a carmine flush along the horizon. The air smells of broken tomato vines.

The strawberries are over. They lasted just as long as I needed them. Now they are safe from my passion.

For these six weeks, you have not waited, in limbo or in hell. You have lived.

You have shown me that the progression is not inevitable.

You have taught me that even if the progression unfolds in its entirety, it can be the tests, the living, the surgery, the living, the chemotherapy, the living, the Damoclean sword, the living, the first metastases, the living, the treatment, the living, the slow progression, the living, through bones, the living, or lungs, the living, or brain, the living, the deathbed, the living while dying, the death, the funeral, the burial, the end, or perhaps the beginning.

Is this what you meant? Is this kind of less-suffering what you meant by no-suffering?

I keep going to Strawberry Hill.

I go for raspberries, for corn and peaches, for harvest apples and melba apples. For tomatoes and new dug potatoes, for carrots tugged from the earth only hours before. For McIntosh and Spies and Ida Reds. Pumpkins.

On the last day of October, the sky is a deep, cold blue. Dark-tinged clouds race across the sun, giving the impression of a light switching on and off over the landscape.

As I lift potatoes into my bag, the winds blow from every side. Caught in the crosscurrents, my orientation is shaken, and I hesitate. The temporary shelter rattles and moans, the straw that bedded the pumpkins swirls crazily against the rackety, wooden wall.

"That's it till next year," says the proprietress, as I present my apples and potatoes to be weighed. She draws closer to the heater.

"We'll be back next June with the strawberries."

Heading for the Millennium:
Seven Easter Stories

Good Friday

ou get up before the rest of the family. Sitting in front of the gas fire drinking coffee and eating twelve-grain bread with strawberry jam, you have serious thoughts. Christmas is when spirit becomes flesh. At Easter, flesh and spirit part company. The approach to Easter is through winter and Lent – cold, introversion, self denial. Good Friday is sacrifice.

Ancient tales teach that sacrifice is how the psyche renews itself. Easter is sacrifice followed by renewal - light, fertility, return to the outside world. (You are assuming a Christian context. Can you assume a Christian context in south central Canada, in 1995?)

Every few minutes, you straighten and look outside. A year ago today, eating breakfast alone on this couch, you saw a procession come along your quiet, tree-lined street. A man staggering under a large wooden cross. Soldiers in tunics. A mob following. No one else (that you talked to, anyway) saw this.

"You saw Christ? Sure you did, Mom," said your teenaged son when he got up. As well as having your serious thoughts and your breakfast, you are realizing there is no procession this year.

Again you wonder whether you could have had a vision.

At noon, your two teenaged sons are still asleep. In the kitchen, your husband is marking papers and cursing students. Suddenly you can't wait to buy a magazine you've heard about, a magazine with an encouraging story; you will walk to the variety store.

Though it's mid-April, the weather is grey and chilly. The swollen oblong heads of the daffodils are still closed; you could have worn your mittens. You come up behind a narrow man with legs like a camel's; he is swaying and talking out loud to himself. Days like this – family times with everything closed, the weather drear – are hard for people who are alone. For an instant you feel just how hard in the quick of your nails, in the premature beat of your heart.

Here in the variety store, which is filled with men whose eyes you take care to avoid, is the magazine. "An Explosion of Green" is the cover story.

Back home, your husband marks on. Your sons sleep on. Time sags like flesh released from a girdle. You once read a story (set in the fifties) about a boy who sprained his wrist getting his girlfriend's girdle off. Your sons don't even know what a girdle is.

In the Philippines, some people have themselves crucified on Good Friday to gain points with God. Those nailing them to the cross use thin aluminum nails, carefully avoid the delicate bones of the palm and the foot. You lay your magazine aside unread, stick cloves in the pink flesh of the ham, carefully avoiding the bones, take the pineapple out of the fridge, pare and chop potatoes, grate cheese, peel apples. Good Friday was once a fast day, a girdle whose eventual shedding made the Easter feast more vivid to the taste buds.

You sprinkle paprika and cheese on the scalloped potato casserole, then you walk over to the table and stand in front of your husband. It is surprisingly long before he looks up at you, his grey-blond hair mussed, pits of marking grief under his eyes.

"I regret the loss of a liturgical calendar," you say to your husband. "I regret living in a culture where the seasons are no longer lived deeply. I regret living at the end of the Christian myth. I regret the general loss of meaning."

Your husband looks at you as if you are a particularly obnoxious student. He shoves the pile of essays across the kitchen table. "Pea brains," he says. "Swine." Your husband believes in karma and reincarnation; you wonder for what unspeakable act this grading is an expiation.

You have just heard there is no such thing as Easter in California. You know that what happens in California happens here ten years later.

Above your head, you hear the shower switch on. It is 1:30 p.m., Good Friday, 1995. Ante Domino. Really Ante Domino. Except in the Philippines.

Easter Baskets

This is the light that rolls over the rim of the world like a rogue wave. Getting out of bed Saturday to sunshine, you decide, in a surge of exuberance, to compose a poem with that thought as the first line. The morning paper has news of murder in Rwanda, slaughter in Grozny, race wars in Europe, fears that Chernobyl will leak again. You wrench your eyes elsewhere, but not before a part of you picks up the bad news and hurries down inside you with it to the rank pond of rotting culture grief that is already sloshing there, threatening to spill over and drown your surges of insouciance, your moments of hope. So often these days you find yourself averting your mind from more evidence of the rotting culture, knowing it has entered you, anyway.

Noon. Your younger son is still asleep. Your oldest is downtown, handing his resumé in to stores in a futile (you suspect) search for a summer job. You dump Easter eggs on your countertop. (This year the boxes in the stores called them Spring eggs.) You know they are pure sugar, bad for your sons' teeth, but you love the innocent colours – chick yellow, apple green, bubblegum pink, baby bonnet turquoise, maiden aunt mauve, clown orange. You have also bought toffees to tuck in the straw: licorice, coffee éclair, raspberry éclair, coconut, brazil nut, menthol, peanut butter, mint, rum. You stand the chocolate bunnies among the candy and run upstairs to where you think you hear your younger son getting out of bed.

"There's a big white bunny with a pink sack in the kitchen. He's in a hurry, looking for two baskets to fill!" (You are hoping for a smile.)

"Sure, Mom, sure. By the way, did Christ stop by yesterday?" You cannot see your son's face because of his shoulder length blonde hair.

"Where are your and Darren's baskets? Darren's downtown."

"I don't know, Mom, on the top shelf of the cupboard maybe, where they are every year?"

"Don't you like getting an Easter basket anymore, Chris?"

"Not as much as you like making it, Mom."

You know this is true. Last Hallowe'en, as a father lifted his fairy queen and his ranger onto your front porch, you realized that it is the parents who keep Hallowe'en going. You and your husband used to slaver on the floor like mendicants, watching Darren and Chris unpack their Hallowe'en loot.

You hide the two baskets in the oven and the shower. Later, as your youngest searches the living room, you venture, "When you were seven or eight, Chris, do you remember asking me whether Santa was real?"

Your son pauses, "No, what did you say?"

"I took you on my lap and kissed your soft little cheek and stated with conviction that Santa Claus was as real as the Easter Bunny." Your son smiles, and for an instant you see the child you have lost forever. Your oldest has just found his basket in the oven. Most of the stores wouldn't even take his resumé. Job hunting sucks, he said when he got home. (You have given up asking him not to say things "suck.")

You dish out four bowls of homemade vegetable soup, slice rough pieces of rye bread. The family gathers round to slurp. *This is the light that pours golden into the corners, unrolls secrets curled like scrolls in the drawers.*

Nuclear Family Drives North to Visit Extended Family

An hour later you are in the car ready to go. The effort of pulling it all together has made your blood hammer your temples. (You assume it is blood; it feels like steel bars.) "There's Jiffy!" says your husband.

You have almost left on an overnight trip with the family cat locked outside. Jiffy is 80, if you count each human year as five cat years. A night outdoors might have finished him off.

A neckless robin with a monstrous orange breast regards you from several different angles as you unlock the back door so Jiffy can brush past your legs into the house. Just as you get back into the car, your son spots a friend and explodes from the other side of your vehicle. The appalling raw intensity of his new voice fills the driveway and street. In the breaks and cracks of this voice you glimpse the world of Dionysus – orgies of drunken satyrs, barefoot maenads suckling wild animals and rending their young limb from limb under a full moon. "Come *on*, Chris," you call.

The way north to your sister's is through Mennonite country. *This is the light that fills the luminous green pastures with morning creatures for whom the world cavort was created.* At the end of many farm lanes are tables of maple syrup jars for sale, tended by small girls in black dresses and black bonnets. Horse-drawn buggies driven by bearded men in black suits drive along the highway shoulders. Luddite that you are, their presence used to comfort you. Then you read a letter in a local newspaper from two English tourists, horrified by the neglected state of the horses' feet, neglect which they claimed would be causing the horses much suffering. Oh yes, your brother confirmed later, those animals are notoriously mistreated.

Now, in this part of the country, instead of comfort you get more grief. You wrench your mind away to the busy yards of the small town you are passing through. *This is the light that impels men and women onto ladders to clean out their eavestroughs and teeter on the ridgepoles of their lives.*

Chris has his walkman turned so loud that you feel its beat in your temples. "Turn it down, *please*," you mouth at your son's earphones, twice, and this flesh of your flesh makes a face and an infinitesimal adjustment to his volume. You try not to notice the rows of long, metal animal factories in the sunny fields.

This is the light that beats blankets, opens trunks, cleans out basements, spreads a life upon a lawn for all to pick over.

Visit to Father in Nursing Home

Your father is in his wheelchair, head hanging and over to one side, like Christ's on the cross. *This is the light that caroms off the heartwood door of sorrow, rousing all within.* Your father does not recognize you or his grandsons. Your mother rises to her feet, her face opening like an Easter lily. Ten minutes later, your sister Rita and your sister-in-law Marie-France bound into the room with Bridget, the tall white poodle. Bridget is wearing a tissue paper flower of purple and yellow on her collar. She growls.

"No dogs allowed," says Chris.

"Bridget is not a dog," says Marie-France. "Don't you see her Easter corsage?"

On the sidewalk outside your father's window, relatives walk those they are visiting along the south wall. *This is the light that moves through the bed-ridden, raises them into tottery bundles supported by sticks along sunny sidewalks.* An old man with a halo of dandelion fuzz hair enters your father's room in his wheelchair. His cheery sentences have all the inflections of English, but make no more sense than the first jargonings of a toddler.

"Well, for Heaven's sake, Mr. Cruickshank, isn't that something!" says your sister, nodding and smiling. Marie-France leans forward, looks from the haloed face to Rita and back again; English is not her first language. When Mr. Cruikshank has wheeled away, Marie-France's brown eyes open wide.

"Does that man have his lucidities?" she asks.

You are still laughing when the nurse enters with your father's four o'clock pill. Bridget growls.

"Why Bridget!" says Marie-France. "That is the first time she ever growls," she says to the nurse. And to look in those wide brown eyes, both human and canine, you would believe it.

You bend to hug your father goodbye, stop in the doorway to take one last look. Through all this, he has been hanging expressionless from the restraint that keeps him in the wheelchair. A line is coming to you from somewhere. William Blake. *Did He who made the lamb make thee?*

Easter Dinner

This is the light that fills the clothes-lines of the world with smacking sheets and flapping, antic desires.

Before dinner at your sister's, you avert your eyes from an article about the dramatically thinned ozone layer and skim one about repetitive strain disease. There is an epidemic of arm, hand, neck and back problems due to people sitting at computer terminals all day. Some people can no longer use their hands even to tie their shoes or carry a cup of coffee. Massaging your right forearm, you obey the summons to table.

Easter dinner is a gourmet feast of barbecued turkey, enchiladas, guacamole, black bean chile, red rice, a hot salad of green and red vegetables. Your son and his twelve year old cousin leave the house between first course and dessert. You will learn later that they walked two blocks to the Corner Grill where they filled up on junk food.

Marie-France pretends to walk Bridget between dessert and coffee. You know that she is outside sneaking a smoke.

Church

It is becoming a family tradition. Since your parents moved back here to the town where they were born and your father went into the nursing home, you, your sister, and your sister-in-law have been going to church with your mother on Easter Sunday. None of you except your mother goes to church the rest of the year.

As usual, when the three of you get all gussied up, you clash. Marie-France is in carmine, Rita is in rose, you are in emerald green. Your mother can be counted on to be in neutral. She can be counted on to give you a last warning to behave before you enter the church.

On the table in front of the pulpit are pots and vases of purple and white and fuchsia hyacinths, yellow daffodils, cream narcissus, white Easter lilies, rosy tulips, purple and white crocus, yellow forsythia. The flowers are in memory of those who have died in the past year. You recognize the names of several people to whom you are distantly related. You decide you will put a plant there for your mother and father when they join the departed.

A tape of muted rock music plays, people talk in supermarket voices, children run in the aisles. The next step will be to install pop machines, you reflect, in case a person feels dry during the sermon. The lights are bright and the reading in the program contains phrases like "you could have fooled me." This is God's house. But it is the same as everywhere else. There is no sense of the sacred, no sense of having entered a space that is Other. What does that say about God, you wonder? That He is no longer divine, no longer transcendent, no longer God? Just a Good Guy who likes His hockey and His beer? Or a Woman? You imagine God having episiotomies and periods and hot flashes. You lean across to your sister-in-law. "Eh bien, Marie-France, did you ever think you'd end up across the ocean in a heathen place like this?"

Marie-France and Rita laugh and your mother gives you a poke: "You said you'd be good."

At least here in the boonies they still sing the old hymns. As the organist plays the familiar chords of *The Old Rugged Cross*, you see the corner of your sister's eye take in you and your mother sharing a hymnbook, singing the words in harmony. You know that your sister is absorbing it, this feeling of belonging to the human family with its bitter-sweet twists and turns, the presence of the transcendent in the sanctuary after all, in the homely beauty of the voices singing the old hymn, in the slanting light entering through stained glass, and she is storing the feeling inside where it will counteract rotting culture grief. You are, too.

"Let us pray," says the minister. You bow your head and let your mind's eye roll over your loved ones, one after the other, like the light that rolls golden into the corners. As it rolls over your sleeping sons, you wish that you had understood in time the difference between spirituality and dogma. You have not fed the part of your sons that needs to know about the world beyond the visible.

Your sister's sun-filled car after church is like a warm nest. Breathing in the familiar fragrance of the women of your family, you indulge in a grand, escalating kertychoo of a sneeze. "Dad will be with us as long as you are," says your sister.

Easter Monday

You are back home. You get up before the rest of the family. Sitting in front of the gas fire drinking coffee and eating twelve-grain bread spread with strawberry jam, you have serious thoughts.

The human condition. The passing of the generation ahead of you. One by one, all the people who have cared about you most in the world. Those who lighten and quicken when you appear, who remember what you did when you were three, or twelve, or thirty-three, who can identify your nose as Aunt Bertha's, your temper as Uncle Ephram's, your crazy streak as your cousin Dorothy's. Those who can see behind the administrator you've become. All will soon be gone. You will miss them for the rest of your life.

Then, like a child presenting flowers to the Queen, the part of you that picks up every sign of the rotting culture steps forward with pansies. A corner of a Mennonite garden you didn't know you noticed until right now, when your unconscious proffers it. Pansies thrive in mitteny April weather, you realize. You can plant some today. You could plant some every Easter Monday.

They were your grandmother's favourite flower because of their faces. Heart's ease, she called them.

As you drive to the Garden Centre, you have a series of memories of your Grandmother. Elizabeth Jane Snell. Lizzy. "Mama" to her children until her death. The brown spot the size of a quarter on her cheek. Her general air of fierce obedience to God the Father no matter how severe the burdens He sent her, and they were severe. Her high voice in church, squeezed off the top of her windpipe, her voice like the sound of grass held between your thumbs and blown on, how she raised it without shame to high "F" and the look in her eyes when she did it, the glazed gleam of a woman submitting with masochistic fervor to her Lord and Master. How you looked up the triangle of her nose that was just like your mother's and your sister's. The sermons re-preached over Sunday lunch. Her breasts lumped under a print housedress, just above her waist, the band in which she wound her pearl-grey hair, her granny glasses, her clacking loose teeth, how she looked in the mornings without her teeth when her hair was loose on her shoulders and her eyes a tender hazel and her breasts unchecked. The furrows in her cheeks, the large bottles of epsom salts waiting in the fridge to purge her with an urgent gush, like a cow's. The ginger ale on picnics, the suppers of bacon and toast and bitter, July lettuce with lacey holes.

By now you have chosen the most beautiful of the pansies and you are back home digging, mixing black soil and peat moss. Your favourites are the periwinkle blue and butter yellow, both with exquisite faces of velvet indigo. Heart's ease, for Elizabeth Jane and for you.

Now you know why you let your five nieces and nephews eat every sweet in the house that time you were in charge of them for a week, why you suggested they denude the cupboards and fridge as soon as their parents were out of sight down the lane, and in one glorious hour consume a week's worth of desserts and treats and bedtime snacks. You did it so that one day in 2045 when you are ashes and dust, one of them will turn to the other and say, "Remember when . . ." and you will rise from the dead as your grandmother has risen today.

Here is the same robin watching you, unable to see a worm in the grass for her beluga belly.

Back inside by the fire, smelling of wet earth, your temples beating with healthy toil this time, you finally read the article in the magazine you bought on Good Friday. The forests of the eastern United States are coming back. Under their regenerating cover, animals long scarce and almost extinct are being sighted in ever greater numbers: coyotes, black bears, wild turkeys, red wolves, cougars, whitetail deer, beaver, moose. The quote that ends the article is the epigraph of naturalist Henry Beston: "Creation is still going on, the creative forces are as great and as active to-day as they have ever been, and to-morrow's morning will be as heroic as any of the world."

Closing the magazine, you recognize your runny nose as joy. It is so long since you read anything that gave you hope for this planet. *This is the light that sends a woman to the woods singing – dangle tin pails from my arms and tap me. The sap you get will cure baldness and impotence, set free spirit trapped in matter, salve the wounds between.*

The Beautiful Sisters in Neydans

*E*very night around eleven, I stagger sated from table to bed. There are no screens on my bedroom window. I lean into lilac-scented air, lean way out in order to slide the peg that releases the heavy wooden shutter. The peg is a little man, his stance stalwart, his expression long-suffering as the *anglaise* fumbles with his upright body. Every night for three nights I grope and scrabble, then give up and call my sister-in-law, Marie-France: "Explain again how you do it."

On the fourth night, I get it. You lay your finger gently underneath *le derrière of M. Le Peg* and tap upwards. *M.* shoots from his slot, and the heavy wooden shutters swing free. You close them against the fragrant air and the church bell, and slide into the cool dark arms of Hypnos.

"When we get to Neydans," says Marie-France, the day before we leave Canada, "I am going to smell. Close my eyes and stand there and just smell."

"What will it be that you smell?" I ask her.

"Home," she says. "It will be the smell of home. I cannot explain it more."

The first time I saw Marie-France Chautemps, I thought that there could not exist on this earth a human being who looked more like a horse. A purebred filly – the lines, the breeding, the thin ankles, the huge brown eyes set wide and shining like dark suns, the high cheekbones tapering into small mouth and chin, the long mane of coarse, curly dark hair braided and coiled in a shining bun. Marie-France would win the Preakness by several lengths, I thought, cross the finish line and toss that fine Gallic head at a field lost in her dust.

We had believed my brother Graham would never marry, for he ate, slept, breathed and talked horses. That Marie-France looked like a horse explained the inexplicable. But when he met Marie, I guess Graham never stopped to ask himself whether this was a woman to take a back seat to a horse.

This is Marie-France's first visit home in five years. She has left her five children behind, I have left my two. For all the years I have known her, Marie-France has been on my territory. Now I am to be on hers.

On our first afternoon, my sister-in-law introduces me to her relatives as *la belle soeur.* "Doesn't that mean 'the beautiful sister?'" I ask her.

Marie-France laughs. "Literally, yes. In France that's what we call her. In Canada, you say the sister-in-law."

So here in France, I am for ten days to be the beautiful sister of Marie-France as Marie-France is the beautiful sister of me.

My brother Graham has our mother's eyes. A strong, yellow-brown, like the heavy soil a bulldozer churns up on a dark, wet day. He has our mother's blood pressure, too. High as the hill behind the old, fourteen room farmhouse that belongs to Graham now. You can see most of Severn county from the top of that hill.

My brother has an eye condition. The doctor says Graham will never be completely blind. He'll always be able to see out of the corner of his eye. When he looks at anything directly, he'll see a black hole. Graham has a white line at the base of his skull, a scar from the operation to remove a growth from his brain. The operation was done at the Hospital for Sick Children in Toronto when he was twenty-one months old.

Five days a week, my brother lives in the city, works for a corporation, dresses in suits and ties. Weekends and summer holidays, he goes to the farm and works like Sisyphus to keep it up, as his father did before him.

"We cannot have a life here, in the city," says Marie-France, "because Graham is always gone on the weekends."

That sentence has for me the familiarity of my face. I heard my mother say it so many times of my father.

We spent our summers on the farm. In those days, it was owned by a relative. Our father inherited it when we were grown up. Now that he is in the nursing home, the farm belongs to Graham.

My mother blamed the farm for everything that was wrong in her marriage. So does Marie-France. My father's heart was not in the city, not in his marriage. His heart was at the farm, with his pure-bred cattle. My brother's heart is there, too, at the farm, with his purebred horses.

It rains all night. In the morning, Marie-France and I go for a walk in the country just outside this tiny village of Neydans, twenty minutes by car from Geneva. In south-western Ontario after a spring rain, the air is redolent with dying earthworms; their ubiquitous corpses stretch full length upon the sidewalks. Here there are no sidewalks and no earthworms, no robins and no squirrels; fat slugs with perky feelers are everywhere underfoot.

Marie-France and I are taking the long way around to the house of *Tante* Marie-Jeanne. Halfway there, the rain begins again. I remove my raincoat and make of it a roof, one side held aloft by me, one by Marie-France. Very soon, my right arm begins to ache and I change to my left. So does Marie-France. Soon we are switching arms every few seconds. "It's surprising how difficult it is to hold one's arms in the air for any length of time," I say to Marie-France.

"*Ah oui,* when I taught at the Toronto French School, that position was used by the teachers as a punishment for disobedient children until a Jewish parent complained. She said it was not appropriate."

I nod, as the significance of arms above the head rolls over me like the raindrops on my coat above – surrender, helplessness, torture. Then, pushing these associations aside – my long ago babies, arms stretched above the head in sleep.

At our farm in Canada, there can be no changes. When the kitchen table is set, the spoons must go in the purple spoon dish in the centre of the table for each person to help himself. They must not be set at each place as is the custom everywhere else.

When we are at the farm, we live out of our suitcases. The clothes of the generations before us fill the drawers. Sweaters and umbrellas from thirty years ago stay on the hallstand at the bottom of the front staircase. The olive green sweater I wore in grade eight hangs in the back washroom over the woodbox.

"I am Graham's wife, but I am not the mistress of this place," says Marie-France. "I am not even a welcome guest."

Marie-France wants to clean out the farmhouse and remodel it. My brother says no. "I might do it, anyway," says Marie-France.

Though we live not far from one another, I write Marie-France a letter, trying to explain what I know Graham cannot put into words and I can say only on paper.

"We lived at the farm only in the summers, Marie-France," I write, "yet the farm felt like our home. Even today, when I step into the old kitchen and take a deep breath – wood smoke, mouse dirt, mold, damp from the cellar floor, old leather, old wood – when I inhale that smell, I get back our childhoods and our departed family members."

"Once, when you were angry, you said, 'It's as if these things are sacred objects.' Well, you were right. They are. There are plenty of other places that are modern and convenient and cleaned out. If we did that to the farm, we'd destroy something of spiritual value – the tradition, the history, the memories of a family."

"Graham is different from you, Marie. Inside you is a sturdiness capable of surviving the vicissitudes of life. That word, "vicissitudes," hisses at Graham. He needs more outer supports than you do."

"When we were children, I remember evenings that seemed charmed. The sun would sit for timeless hours on the west horizon, a huge red pomegranate that promised another day of perfect summer weather. Those August evenings, the soft, humid air would be scented with Astrachan apples and pink antique roses in their second bloom. Our aunt would come across the creek, up the hill and around the gravel path to the side door. She'd have a sealer of bluish milk in her hands, still warm from the cow, and she'd sit on the stone step beside our mother while Graham and I played behind the banks of purple and white phlox. When the first bat dipped and turned above us, we'd all go inside."

"All I have to do to bring that back is to step inside the farmhouse, and smell. The smell of the farm is the smell of home. I think Graham needs it to get through his life. Maybe I do, too."

"Try to understand, Marie-France. To you, it's just an old, inconvenient house; a hilly, stony, one hundred acres. To us, it's home."

Four roads lead into the village of Neydans, and all four roads end at the church.

Open the church door and you are in the presence of Other. Cool, dim hush – an authority that is not of this world. The church is the heart of the village. On the top of the church steeple is the *coq.*

The church bell rings every hour. One clang for one o'clock. Two clangs for two o'clock. And so on. Except at seven in the morning, seven in the evening, and noon. Then the bell becomes animated and peals an intricate and lengthy tale.

"What's that?" I ask Eliane, Marie-France's aunt, who is giving us a home for ten days.

"That is the bell for the *Angélus,* she tells me. Three times a day, the church bell tells us it is time to stop what we are doing. Attend, and say a prayer. Remember that Jesus Christ was made flesh and lived for a time as a man on this earth."

"There is another sound the church bell makes," adds my beautiful sister. "An odd note, coming at the end. When you hear that, you know someone in the village has died."

Five members of Marie-France's family have died since her last visit here. "One day soon I will be going to the cemetery," she says.

"Would you like me to come with you?" I ask.

"No, I will make that journey alone."

My mother felt sick when she saw the swollen purple birthmark on the back of Graham's head; from day one she worried that it would affect his intelligence or his physical abilities. During her absence in Toronto for the operation, I began kindergarten. I was four years old.

A neighbour took me the first day, and after that, I walked alone, a distance of several city blocks. Along the way were houses set back from the street, bushes crowded close to their windows. Monsters lived in those houses, ogres hunched beneath the manhole covers.

In those days, the mother was not allowed to stay with the child, was not allowed even to visit the child after surgery.

For two weeks, our mother watched her young son through the one way mirror, his white face and bandaged head, his lower lip extended and trembling as he looked around the strange white space. She wasn't allowed to go in and she didn't go in.

"How could you not have gone in?" I ask her. When my sons were sick, I slept on their floor.

"I know how it must seem to you now," she answers. "But to us, in those days, doctors and nurses and hospitals were Gods."

Back when my brother was still single, he had many car accidents. We always said he should stick to his horse and buggy. Then, four years ago, Graham climbed a tree in the back yard of the house in the city where he lives with Marie-France and their five kids. The tree's roots were in the plumbing and Marie-France had been nagging him for months. While he was sawing off a limb, the branch he was holding snapped back and knocked him to the ground, wrecking his knee. Three operations later, the doctor told him it would never be any better.

It's hard for Graham to ride a horse now. He blames Marie-France.

Tante Marie-Jeanne is eighty-three years of age. She is the sister who never married; there was one in almost every family. Marie-Jeanne is the last surviving Chautemps of her generation.

Marie-Jeanne is tiny. Her head bobs incessantly, as if her neck were a spring. Her eyes are red, red-brown of newly turned clay. She wears layers of clothing that look as if they are part of her body, as if they do not come off at bedtime and on in the morning, but rather mold themselves to her angles, absorb and release the smells and secretions of her body like an animal's fur. Her garden is the size of a large city lot. The fingers and backs of *Tante* Marie-Jeanne's hands are cross hatched by lines of ingrained soil. Toil made visible.

Her kitchen has a dirt floor. Cold, age, earth, faintly bitter smell of burnt wood of *épiceur* rise to meet us as we enter. With her live the animals. A black and white dog. A marmalade cat. Mice and spiders. Cows. The house and the barn are under one roof. Mooings, smells, and bovine chewings are part of the texture of her days and nights.

The bachelor son, Riri, lives here, too. Marie-France remembers the spring a bird flew through the open upstairs window and built a nest in Riri's bedroom. Every evening, Riri cleaned up the bits of straw and mud and bird dirt. It would not have occurred to him to disturb the nest.

Here in *La Haute Savoie,* the *coq* of Marie-Jeanne roams free. He chases children, inflicts wounds. Hens cross the yard with that dainty, pernickety step I had forgotten. The lowest hen in the pecking order has lost the feathers from more than half of her body. As we emerge from *Tante's* cold kitchen into warm May sunshine, this hen jitters and flutters across my path, causing me to stumble. "You dumb cluck," I say aloud.

Marie-France raises her eyebrows. Even after twenty years in Canada, there are expressions she has not heard.

When my mother was finally allowed, after two weeks, to take my brother from the Hospital for Sick Children, he wouldn't look at her. Wouldn't speak. My mother talked and talked, trying to bring back the life he knew before these two weeks of strangers and pain. Finally she started to talk about his big sister.

Graham looked up at her and smiled. "Sis-ter," he said.

When she arrived home at last, my mother told me: "They had to go right to the base of Graham's brain."

I saw a single file of men in white coats trekking across a stark land of fearsome splendour over which loomed a mountain – Graham's beleaguered brain.

A few years ago, my brother went to France. He made his speeches in Paris, then travelled to the town of Annemasse on the eastern border where Marie-France's parents live. Marie-France's mother had knit for the children leggings, coats, sweaters, jumpsuits, hats, mitts. She knit them in primary colours, in the French style. At the Geneva airport, Graham set down his briefcase and suitcase to dial a number.

When he turned around, the suitcase was gone. Two years of loving toil by Marie-France's mother. Marie-France blamed Graham.

Rows of trees and high enclosing fences surround the straight rows and clipped grass. This French cemetery is a woman in a corset or a soldier at attention.

The small Canadian cemetery I know best is a blowsy woman with her tresses undone, a wooden soldier propped against a fence. Graves are overgrown with long grass, and cattle wander among the windfalls. Many tombstones in the cemetery I know best hold the names of people who are still alive. The birth date is filled in, the date of death left blank.

To have your name already on your tombstone and your tombstone already in your cemetery is not the custom here in France. In this country, the only people with their names on tombstones are the ones lying underneath.

When I lie down at the east end of this cemetery and roll onto my left side, I can see Lake Geneva in the distance. Geneva. Neutrality, refuge for persecuted Protestants, The International Red Cross, the World Health Organization. From here I can see the farm that is half in Switzerland, half in France. Now again I picture my beautiful sister and I in the rain, arms up. The image wavers, and the two in the rain, arms up, are hunted figures discovered half a kilometer from safety. Here is where the Jews crossed the border from France into Switzerland during the war.

When I try to get out of *le cimetière*, I cannot open the gate. I have lain so still among the dead of Neydans, lain so long looking into the face of Geneva, that the keepers thought me gone; they have finished their work and locked the graveyard behind them.

If I stand here inside the spiked iron fence and cast my *au secours* into this vasty green valley, will my cry be heard and recognized for what it is – a daydreaming Canadian locked inside a French cemetery – or will the bent villagers go on planting potatoes in the red-brown soil and weeding the vineyards on the sunny slopes, thinking me but a spirit who rails against her untimely entombment?

The gate swings open, its "lock" turning out to be nothing but my usual ineptitude with my hands. "Tell me about it!" says M. LePeg, rolling his eyes.

One winter day in Canada, Marie-France tells me she has only half a face. She tells me she is all eyes and nose. She has no mouth and no chin. I tell her she is beautiful. She shakes her head.

Her words follow me. I cannot forget them.

Two weeks later I get a call. Marie-France has been taken to hospital by her best friend, Janey. Janey says Marie-France is suicidal.

I am there later that day, but Marie-France has already been released with a prescription for an anti-depressant. I find her sitting on the living room couch beside her terrier, Patsy.

Marie-France looks white and small and alone; the five kids are at Janey's. Graham is scrubbing the kitchen floor. I give Marie-France a long hug and send Graham off to bed, make coffee and bring it to the living room. I set the tray down and hug her again.

"Marie-France, what happened?" I ask, through sudden tears. "Don't you know we couldn't get along without you?"

"I don't know what happens. All of a sudden I know I am trapped and can never get away. I am running from my devils for many years, and now they are catching me. If I get out of my chair I will go to the bathroom and swallow every pill. I phone Janey instead."

"But why, Marie-France? What about the children?"

"I know. I don't feel like that now. But I am afraid it will come back. Graham says he will clean out the drawers at the farm and put the clothes in the attic."

"Oh, Marie-France." I reach for her and our tears fall together. A week later, I visit again, and Marie-France asks her questions.

"What have I done? Where do I belong? Where I am going now?"

Back home, I phone my sister-in-law with an idea. "Marie-France, let's go home. You haven't been back in five years. I'll go with you, meet your family."

In the end, everyone agrees that Graham will look after the children with the help of a neighbour, and Marie-France and I will go to Neydans in May.

The day before our departure, Graham phones me, talks about this and that. I ask him about his recent appointment with the eye doctor. Yes, he confirms, he has lost more of his vision and the doctor has told him he must make changes, reduce the stress in his life. Only when I tell Graham I have to go does he clear his throat.

"Do what you can to help save the marriage," he says.

My first memory is Graham.

It is the twenty-eighth of November. I am three years old, this very day. My fair hair is in four braids, two wound round my head as crown, two hanging to my shoulders. I stand at the top of a flight of high, narrow stairs.

My mother comes into view carrying a tiny form wrapped in blue. My new brother. I have not seen my mother for a week. I am about to begin a rapturous descent of the stairs.

Onto my shoulder descends a heavy hand, the hand of my mother's mother. It jerks me back, away from the stairs. "Stay still and be quiet. Your mother has her hands full with the new baby."

That tiny form wrapped in blue, those words, that hand. My first memory.

When Marie-France and I have been in Neydans one day, I realize that I have not truly known her, but now it will be possible. Here are her eyes and her hair, there her nose and her laugh. These variations and mutations of her features are her mother and her father, those are her brothers and sisters, her cousins and aunts and uncles. And here is her habit of lengthening and drawing back her chin when she makes an ironic remark, of puffing out her lips when she is fed up. Here is the country lane where she spent her childhood, the old farm kitchen and sitting room that was her home. The vineyard of her grandfather. The mountain that watched over her. The graveyard of her ancestors.

Neydans is familiar to me on sight because I have known Marie-France.

And now I understand as I have never understood how much a part of a person is her country and her family.

Here, I am the stranger. Without language, I do not recognize myself. With language enough to express only the pedestrian, to understand only one person at a time, I am without my flights of animation and humour. Stolid as a tree trunk I sit among these lively, gregarious relatives and friends of my beautiful sister. When they laugh, I am silent and unresponsive. Their smiles turn naturally to include me, then dim at my blank expression. My presence has the wet blanket effect. I appear, even feel, serious and stupid.

"Pourquoi elle ne parle pas comme nous?" three-year-old Jessica asks her parents.

Suddenly I remember Marie-France's sister who visited us in Canada several years ago. Nathalie spoke no English. She sat among us like a suitcase. I dismissed her as dull and humourless. Now I am Nathalie.

We are eating dinner outside at the home of Marie-France's brother, René. A cousin is here with his young wife, Marine. They have a twenty-month baby and a four-month baby. Near the end of the main course, Marine rolls up her sweater and takes her bare breast in her hand. She inspects it, rummages for a napkin and dusts it off, finishing her pasta with her right hand while her left holds her breast ready and naked. She might as well be exposing a hangnail for all the interest anyone takes in her breast.

Another day, we visit a beach in Annecy. Breasts lolling at waistlines, breasts stabbing the air at the level of the heart, breasts dangling near bellybuttons, breasts pert as ice cream cones licked to a point. A slim, blond girl who looks like my fifteen-year-old niece wades into the water holding hands with her boyfriend. She is wearing only a string of bikini at her hips. My shoulders contract in an unsophisticated, new world wince!

Yes, it is a new experience for me to sit at table with a large, mute, leaking breast as just one more dinner guest. No matter where I look, the nipple seems to be there, following me, like the moon on an evening stroll.

This past winter I grew out of my jeans, so in the spring, I buy a new pair to wear in France. As usual, they fit me around the waist but are too big for my hips and rear end. So what, I decide! They're comfortable. We'll be mostly in the country.

But there is something in me that rebels against going to the fashion capital of the world in jeans that do not fit. I tell this self to be quiet; I tell her she is foolish and vain. But she nags and nags, like a child whining for candy in a supermarket, and, like the mother who finally gives in at checkout, I hurry to the alterationist at the last minute.

One evening, Marie-France and I end up in a lakeside apartment in the beautiful resort of Annecy. The apartment belongs to Marie-France's Aunt Thérèse and Uncle Jacques, a sophisticated pair who have travelled the world. I am wearing my jeans.

The bell rings. It is Véronique, the daughter, come to dine with us. Véronique is as chic as a Vogue fashion model. She kisses everyone on both cheeks, then points out to her father that he is dressed in checks and plaids. Jacques hurries to change his shirt.

"What do you do?" Marie-France asks Véronique later, as Thérèse brings to the table a stunning still life of seafood and steamed vegetables.

"I own a company that markets a line of designer jeans," says Véronique, with a flick of her elegant, Gallic wrist.

"Oh la-*la!*" says the voice of my foolish self. "To think you almost ended up here tonight in jeans that sagged from your derrière. Maybe you'll listen to me after this!"

There is a supermarket in St. Julien. There is a brand new air conditioned mall with hundreds of stores in Annemasse. There is a McDonald's. The mall and the McDonald's are full of people. The main street of the town is empty. There is a supermarket at the edge of the small alpine village through which we pass to go to Marie-France's brother's chateau.

Marie-France's aunt and godmother still go to the little stores every day for that day's food. Their daughters work outside the home. They go to the *supermarché* on Saturday and buy groceries for a week.

There is a pizzeria on the main road one kilometre from Neydans. It is full every evening. Neydans was surrounded by country twenty years ago. Now there is a house every little way.

"The France you knew and loved is disappearing," I tell Marie-France. "The new world is swallowing the old."

"No," my beautiful sister shakes her dark head. "Never."

On our second to last day, Eliane recounts to us her dream of the night. Two people, they are women she thinks, come to her house.

They are rummaging through her drawers, doing her housework, eating her food. "Oh la-la!" laughs Eliane. "It was so silly!"

As she tells this, I remember Carl Jung's idea that one of the functions of dreams is to compensate for our waking attitude. On some level, is this hospitable Eliane experiencing Marie-France and me as an invasion?

Mentally I stick out my tongue at this thought. No wonder if she is, Vivian. Here you are after ten days, presuming even to analyze her dreams!

Au marché in Annemasse, near the end of our stay, the animals one buys to eat are alive. Rabbits, hens, geese. Snails oozing forth from their enclosing, spiral shells. The French do not share our squeamishness at putting our hatchet where our mouth is.

An oddly familiar figure scurries around a corner and past me. It is Marie-France's mother. I am the only one to see her, and for an instant I consider whether or not to tell Marie-France. I do. They stand and talk briefly. Today Marie-France's mother does not have on her made-up, company face; she looks old and tired. Neither mother nor daughter suggests going for *un café*.

We have seen Marie-France's parents only once, though they are a scant fifteen minutes away and though an ocean has separated them from their daughter for five years. Somehow I had hoped that this journey home might be one of reconciliation for Marie-France, had even dreamed of myself as her shield and her peacemaker. That evening, my beautiful sister tells me for the first time the whole story of her youth, ending with how, when she was twelve, she tried to drown herself in the river. I lean my head against hers; the strands of my straight blond hair mingle with her dark curls.

On one of our last evenings in Neydans, Marie-France and I find ourselves alone in Eliane's back yard, the rest of the family momentarily elsewhere. We begin talking about Graham, and Marie-France describes his arrival home from work each evening.

"He comes in the door and he says *bonjour*. I say hi. He asks me why I speak English. He goes into the bedroom, takes off his long pants, drops his shirt in the laundry. He goes to the basement in his underpants and puts on his jeans. He comes upstairs and takes the top off the pot and smells it. 'What's for dinner? he says. Oh, I had that at lunch, he says.' He gets the mail from the spot where it always sits, and opens it."

"We have a dining room table. There is not room for all. When everybody is home, the family sits around the table, and I am at my own small table. One time we have a big fight about getting a new table. I want a table with boards so we can adjust the size. Graham wants a table that is one long solid block. We cannot agree. So we still have the table that is too small."

"Did you really know what you were doing, Marie-France, at age twenty-three, giving up your country, coming to the new world to marry a stranger?" I ask her.

"No, I did not. It was an adventure. I wanted to get away. I did not know then that even an ocean between me and certain devils will not separate us. I did not know that a country can be like a mother. There has been so much pulling me back, so much that I longed for. But this week, *ma belle soeur*, I receive a shock. I realize that I no longer belong here, either. These twenty years away have changed me. I am – how do you say it – not fish and not bird."

"Neither fish nor fowl."

"That's it, exactly. That's how I feel."

"Marie-France, why don't you put the two youngest at your little table, and you sit at the big table with the rest of the family, Graham at one end, you at the other."

"Why?"

"Something like that is important. It sends a message."

"I agree, but that's how it seems to be. Me at the little table by myself."

She looks away, at the row of lilac trees in bloom. The dark suns glow with a knowledge that cannot be shared.

After ten days among the people of my beautiful sister, I am transformed from guest into one-of-the-family, from *anglaise* to *belle famille.* As I undergo this metamorphosis, each person brings his or her treasure.

Tante Eliane, of the forget-me-not eyes, hands Marie-France and me a videotape. It is a play. Shy, retiring Eliane has the starring role. Her dormant self, now sprung to life in this *drame*, is strident, persistent, spectacularly stupid. At the climax of the play, she mistakes a voting booth for a toilet, defecates therein and presents her product on the white ballot to the Deputy Returning Officer. The audience of local people screams in mirth.

Marie-France's sister, Nathalie, who is nothing like a suitcase, whose eyes are the gold of the burned down crust of fondue, brings out a photograph album filled with pictures of her dog. Marie-France's godmother shows the cage full of snails she carefully tends in her back yard.

Eliane's husband, Guy, is the most retiring, the most *fermé*, of *la famille Chautemps*. On our last day, Eliane brings out X-rays of Guy's wrist. Guy asked her to show them, she says. His wrist is not like ours, she explains. There are metal pins replacing parts of his bone. Now he has no pain. Together, my beautiful sister and I hold the X-rays up to the light and exclaim at this new and remarkable wrist.

As I acknowledge the treasures that are brought to me one by one by this, my newly discovered *belle famille*, I find myself musing. Have I always recognized the treasure of others? Have I accorded it the respectful attention it deserves? For treasure sometimes appears in the guise of a turd on a piece of paper.

On the last evening, it is spitting rain. No, the French do not say "spitting" of rain, Marie-France tells me. Eighty-three year old Marie-Jeanne comes to Eliane's door with a packet for Marie-France. No, she will not stay. She has left the dog alone. Marie-France and I step outside with her despite the rain.

Tante Marie-Jeanne's bicycle is tall and modern. She hops aboard, ready to let it carry her away. She wears no helmet for this ride. Just as she sets off, the evening *Angélus* sings forth. As her great-aunt disappears around the curve in the gravel road, Marie-France turns to me. Are those raindrops or tears on her eyelashes? My beautiful sister is without words and we stand arm in arm, listening, as the final note of the *Angélus* dies away in the twilight.

The Sun is Out, Albeit Cruel

*T*he day Marie-France makes her announcement, the whole family is together, in Rilling, Ontario. In the morning is Canada's birthday parade. I'm not thinking about Marie-France; when the float of old folks from the Bonnie Brae Nursing Home chugs by, my first thought is that when our m om sees it coming, she'll worry that our dad is on it. Up there on display in the annihilating July sun, the old folks are so white they look as if they've been let out for recess from Hades. All of them are hunched and staring ahead with the look of a dog enduring a hose bath, except that it's sun coming at them with penetrating, pressure cooker force. Our dad's not there, of course.

Following the Bonnie Brae wagon is a float of rubbery clowns lolloping up and down on their small moving stage. The clowns are pink and genial, proudly oozing sweat and flinging suckers to the crowds of July first holidayers. HOME FOR THE TRAINABLE RETARDED reads the sign on the back of their wagon.

I'm on my bum on the curb, bare legs straight, my straw hat a futile shield against the fierce sun. A horse wearing blue jeans shies back and high steps sideways; its rider trains a water pistol on us. On one side of me is my sister, Rita, on the other my sister-in-law,

Marie-France, her long, thick mane gone, her curly hair now short and spritzer saucy. The three of us open our mouths and spread our arms. "More, more," we holler, at the water pistol man.

Spoils are tossed our way. With my two kids and my five nieces and nephews, I plunge repeatedly onto hot asphalt, skinning my palms to snatch toffees and bubblegum, magic markers and pencils, suckers and ballpoints and black jawbreakers.

At the end of our row of family sit my husband, Steve, and my brother, Graham. Graham's shaved his beard since I saw him last. He's shaking his head at me in disgust for fighting his kids for treats in the asphalt trenches. The new-found skin of his cheek and jaw looks like bark on the forest floor when you turn it over and the slugs scatter, when it still holds that damp film of stilly cool.

I lean against my sister: "Despite the heat, our brother doth give off a clammy air."

Rita pokes me and giggles as the Royal Canadian Legion blares by, their float manned by a score of navy uniformed seniors standing straight as cedar fence posts. The faces under wool tams are puce poppies of pride and incipient stroke.

Again we topple together, knock heads in mock jackanape clumsiness. We are on holiday. The sun is out, albeit cruel. We are in silly putty mode.

I remember the day Marie-France discovered that Graham's surname, Kerr, was identical in sound to the word for surly dog. "It describe him perfectly," she said, a cruel beam in her brown eye. That was soon after Yves was born. Yet she and Graham went on and on: Bernard – merde, another boy; Eliane – enfin, a daughter; Guy – yet another boy; Annelise – a last girl to look after Maman in her old age.

We Kerrs shook our heads at this folly. Why did they do it? Did they think big family meant big happy?

"Yes, and pigs might fly, too," Grandma Kerr was heard to say.

Sometimes, when we're by ourselves, my sister and I talk about Marie-France. How beautiful she is, how French. How, when we're depressed, we can feel better as soon as she walks into the room. How we can't imagine our family now without her.

Canada's birthday parade over, we're on our way to the nursing home to visit my dad.

"Dettol, pee, shit, ennui." I sing the words to Marie-France. "It's taken me years to identify it – the smell in Bonnie Brae. Years. After I've been in to visit, it follows me home and wraps itself around my dreams."

My sister-in-law nods. "Your hair is great," I add, taking my eyes from the road to admire her again. "So chic, so French." We pull off the gravel road and stop in front of the new building that withers in a treeless field just outside Rilling. I let my forehead thump to the padded wheel of the Honda. "I hate to leave this air. Please go into his room ahead of me. Those few seconds before he sees us are the worst."

Even now, Marie-France gives no sign that this day will be different from dozens of others we Kerrs have spent together. She walks ahead and presses the buttons inside the doors of Bonnie Brae. The heat in the hall is as torrid as on the sunny asphalt path outside. We head for my dad's room.

Marie-France enters first. My dad is slumped in his wheelchair. Marie-France zip-a-dee-doo-daws around the room, straightening and fluffing and animating. Take even a room like this, she can rev it up a few levels, whereas I can feel myself glub glubbing in the dettol-pee quagmire before I'm even through the door.

But today, not even his daughter-in-law can rouse my dad. He's slumped over, focused on his sleeve.

"Never mind about that, Lewis," says Marie-France, several times, rubbing my dad's almost helpless hands with her warm ones; but as soon as he's left to himself, his right hand comes up to his left sleeve and works away. He's trying to grasp one of the coarse white flecks of wool that stand out from the weave of his sweater. We give up trying to get his attention, and the two of us sit on the end of the bed and chat.

Eventually, Marie-France goes down the hall to find a local paper and I to use the washroom. Returning, I catch the moment when, after an hour of attempting to grip the fleck between his crippled thumb and index finger, my dad succeeds in pulling it off. I survey the prize, which stands at attention for inspection on his finger, like the legionnaires.

This is the stuff of *The Guiness Book of Records*. Or the Commonwealth Games. (At the moment, they're having an unseemly public tiff over whether Disabled Athletes will be included in future.) *And this just in,* I imagine the announcer saying, *from Bonnie Brae Nursing Home in the hamlet of Rilling, Ontario. A man who has suffered an eighteen-year route by Parkinson's disease succeeded this afternoon in gripping and removing a fleck of wool from his sweater. Lewis Kerr's daughter, interviewed just before airtime, expressed the hope that the fleck would be preserved in the Disabled Athletes' Hall of Fame, soon to be constructed in Victoria at a cost of 1.5 billion tax payer dollars.*

"Why don't we see headlines about these achievements?" commented Ms Kerr. *"Here is where the real dramas are being enacted."*

"You have the silliest look on your face, Vivian." Marie-France reappears in the doorway just as I'm handing the mike back to the reporter. "Come on, we have to get going."

I zoom in from never-never land, focus my eyes and stand up. "I was on TV," I tell her.

My dad neither lifts his head nor looks at us as we kiss him goodbye and leave him to his sleeve. In my gut is the familiar twist of guilt and relief as the front door of Bonnie Brae closes behind us.

Rilling is semi-circled by a wide, deep apostrophe of water, the Sanasateen River. Across from the park, where it flows deepest and widest, is where my sister Rita lives. One minute the Sanasateen holds the changing world of the sky, the next, it repels reflection with its wrinkles, waves, and ruffles. Rita's backyard slopes gently down to the reeds, cattails, sedge, and rushes of the Sanasateen's banks. On the old cement bridge is a sign that would never have escaped the standardizing stamp of a city bureaucrat:

NO LEAPING, JUMPING, VAULTING, SPRINGING, PLUNGING, DIVING, OR CATAPULTING FROM THIS BRIDGE.

"I was so afraid they'd have your dad up on that float," says my mother when we stop by to pick her up, "that when I saw it coming my heart nearly stopped." She places her hand on her heart. "Imagine them putting Betty O'Hanlon and Violet Grey up there. They looked downright cranky."

"Lewis was fully occupé in his own room, Grandma Kerr," says

Marie-France, winking at me as she moves the takeout box of empty coffee cups and helps my mother into the front seat for the short drive to my sister's.

As we glide along Rilling's back streets, I count one, two, three diminutive black men holding lanterns above glistening lawns of Weed and Feed green. The ornaments are highlighted by spikes of the merciless July sun. "What are you gawking at, Vivian?" says my mother.

"Oh, everything and nothing – the look of a summer day in Rilling, Ontario."

"Well, keep your eyes on the road."

I stop the car in front of my sister's place and the three of us slowly descend the slope towards Rita, who's ankle deep in the Sanasateen pulling on the anchor of her rowboat. Up the river a little way, the teens of Rilling are being catapulted from the cement bridge by their own uncontrollable energy; they're flying, really, aloft and omnipotent for a glorious instant against the burning blue sky. They land with a splash that rocks the Sanasateen against its banks.

Two of my mother's grandchildren are in the water – Eliane and Annelise. As we round the tangle of willow, we see them swimming away from us, across the river towards Rilling. The sleek, receding heads look as if they belong to two otters.

It's a shortcut to town," shrugs my sister, "they didn't want to go around by the bridge."

Oh la la, that sun, he is hot!" exclaims Marie-France, bending over to splash river water on her newly bared neck.

"What have Eliane and Annelise got on?" says my mother, still watching her granddaughters' progress across the river.

"Their clothes – shorts and T-shirts," shrugs Rita again. "Anyhow," she adds, splashing water on her face and stepping out of the river, "I have something to tell you. Hell Bent For Election is dead."

Hell Bent is Graham's best horse, the one he had such hopes for, the gelding with the white star out of Forked Lightning. "He had an accident in Linda Blair's stable," Rita continues. "Graham had him there to have work done on his feet. Hell Bent got tangled in a rope and strangled. That's why Graham was clammy, as you put it, Vivian, at the parade. He found out just before he came."

"How could that happen?" asks our mother.

Again Rita shrugs. "Linda Blair couldn't understand it. She said a horse couldn't do that if it tried. She was really upset!" As Rita speaks, I picture Linda Blair's bony face, imagine her bending forward to kiss the dead horse on his soft nose.

"So Graham's horses are suicidal now, I guess," says Marie-France. Again I see the cruel beam in the brown eyes. Rita gives her a mock slap. But as usual Marie-France has made us laugh.

"Poor Graham," says Grandma Kerr.

Poor Graham indeed, I think, looking at my chic and feisty sister-in-law in her new hair. I'm only too aware that for a Chautemps, Kerr now may not mean Kerr forever. Still, I'm not prepared for what Marie-France will announce later this afternoon.

Marie-France is fond of telling a certain story about her oldest son, Yves. But the story is not really about Yves. It's about Kerrs, about us, the family to which Marie-France Chautemps has found herself joined by marriage.

On the day in question, Marie is sitting on the front steps of her home north of Toronto, picking over raspberries. Around the corner of the suburban street comes her twelve-year-old son. At his mother's request, he's been walking Patsy, the family's Jack Russell terrier.

Yves approaches, his left hand holding the leash handle, the leash sliding behind him, an empty collar tumbling and skipping at its end. There is no dog.

Marie-France stands up. She plants her right hand on her hip, with her left she shields her eyes from the sun. "Where is Patsy?" she hollers. (Patsy is her sixth child.) "Where's Patsy?" she hollers again, though Yves is now turning in at the front sidewalk.

It takes this second shout from his mother for Yves to return to earth and focus his eyes. "Patsy?" he says.

"Yes, Patsy, *mon gar*, where she is?"

Yves turns around and looks at the empty collar.

"She's not here." He looks up at his mother. "I didn't know she wasn't here."

Marie-France looks heavenward and crosses herself. "Yves!" she says, coming off the porch and putting her face a lemon's length from her son's, "how you can not know she gets away? It take a hell of a lot of wiggling and twisting for Patsy to get out of her collar!"

Yves produces a baffled shrug. Then there is a yip and a clip clipping of nails on cement as Patsy rounds the corner and trots purposefully towards her mother.

At this point the incident loses drama and settles into its place near the top of Marie-France's extensive repertory of stories.

Yes, Yves is a Kerr, not a Chautemps, as Marie-France often points out. He is one of us: a slack-jawed, wool-gathering, belly-breather, his inner world so compelling that for long periods of time the outer ceases to exist. And Marie-France, who is by nature as warming, as outgoing, as life-giving as the sun, has found herself in a swamp of introverts whose ways are as mystifying and as maddening as anything she has ever encountered.

On our way to the park across the river, by car, my mother gestures to the take-out box and says isn't it nice that they have a hole now in the plastic lid of a cup of coffee so you can drink it with a straw. Marie-France says that the hole is to sip from. My mother says it's for a straw. *Insists* on it. I cross my eyes at Marie and she rolls hers at me.

Across the bridge, we disembark and lock the car. We're going to buy tickets for the duck race. First duck to cross the finish line brings the ticket owner $500. Grandma Kerr safely out of earshot, Marie-France grabs me by the elbow: "With Grandma Kerr for a mother, is it any wonder your brother ask me why I put on perfume to go play badminton when what I'm spraying on my neck is insect repellent!" She laughs, "Good Lord, Vivian. Hot coffee with a straw! Can you imagine?"

I take her arm. "Marie-France, when will you realize that we Kerrs are baffled by the workings of the physical world? I know it's hard for a Chautemps to understand, but such things are mysteries to us!" I gesture at my mother who is walking ahead with Rita. "Remember, this is the woman who made coffee from wiener water that was quietly minding its rank business on the back burner. I mean, why run fresh when that in the saucepan will do?"

"Oh, Vivian," giggles my sister-in-law, "I forgot that one. That was a good one." She gives my arm a squeeze and we follow Rita and my mother across the park. Their progress is slow. Living here, Rita knows half the people at the duck race.

"Look, Vivian," Marie-France is pointing at the bridge. There are no teenagers in sight now. Instead, a dump truck is edging towards the cement railing. The back of the truck tilts slowly upwards and, with the escalating thunder of an avalanche, five hundred yellow, rubber duckies slide into the Sanasateen River.

Once in the water, the ducks' progress is slow, and people again begin visiting with one another and lining up for cold drinks. Marie-France and I find a shady spot under a willow and I spread my green, summer shawl for us to sit on.

It's then Marie-France makes her announcement. When I raise my head, those bright, brown eyes are full upon me.

"Well, Vivian, I think you have guessed," she says quietly.

"Guessed? No, what is it, Marie?"

"I'm getting out, Vivian."

"Out? What do you mean?"

"Separation. I'm leaving your brother."

"But Marie-France, we've talked about this before, don't say it again, please. You know I can't imagine our family without you."

"Well, you will have to start imagining it."

She's said this before, but only in a rage. This afternoon, she is calm and there is a sadness at the centre of her bright, dark eyes. These words have not washed from her on a gush of emotion. They've been sorted and weighed and measured; they sit on a foundation that is not going to disappear.

I move closer and give her a hug. "Marie, I know how it must seem, but try to understand. Graham loves horses, but he loves you, too. In his own way."

She nods, staring now at the drifting yellow ducks. "I mean it, Vivian. I told your brother last night. It is not just the horses coming first; we have many more troubles. You know that."

"What did Graham say?"

"He refuse to discuss."

I look at over at my sister-in-law. Several speeches go through my head:

Marie-France, your troubles aren't really Marie/Graham troubles, they're Kerr/Chautemps troubles. But Kerrs need Chautemps.

The Sun is Out, Albeit Cruel

And Chautemps need Kerrs, believe it or not. It's hard for the sun to talk to the moon; it's hard even to see the moon when the sun is out. But where would we be without both?

That speech is no good. It's Kerr talk.

Marie-France, someday your duck will come in.

Ah oui, bien sûr, she'd say.

Marie-France, without you, we Kerrs will drown in the dettol-pee quagmire.

Then get a gill, she'd say.

"Marie-France, can you imagine how the roof of a person's mouth would look after drinking coffee through a straw? All those little red, burnt circles – smarting like hell!"

She laughs. Throws back that elegant Chautemps head of hers and laughs. But that's only for now, and I know it. I look around the park. Though the sun is as fierce and as bright as ever, though a grand covey of yellow duckies floats serenely down the Sanasateen, I'm covered with hundreds of sharp little shiver prickles.

That night, we feast on Rita's barbecued chicken, baked potatoes, and strawberry shortcake. For the twelve mile drive to the farm, six Kerrs squeeze into my car: Graham, Yves, my husband Steve, our sons, Darren and Chris, me at the wheel. I drive slowly, windows down, high beams lighting a stretch of gravel road ahead. Soft country air on our burnt red faces. Crickets, frogs, the crunch of tires on gravel, an occasional stone pinging against metal. Dark shadows, the black sky, a moon one night away from full. Smell of the Sanasateen. No one says a word. This is Kerr country.

When I coast down to the farmhouse fence and turn off the car, we sit for a moment, still under the spell of the night. Then the van with Marie-France at the wheel rounds the stone wall, radio rocking, Patsy yipping, horn beeping, kids at every window.

"Hey, over there, are you every last one dead?" yells the driver. "Sitting like how-do-you-say zombies in the dark!"

The next morning, Graham and I drive over to our cousin Alec's to get a flat of strawberries.

The sun this July morning is a flasher, sprinting ahead of Graham's old, red pickup truck. As my brother and I bounce over the gravel road at high speed, we create mighty halos of dust for all within our span. This morning, Marie-France's words seem like so much dandelion fuzz. I know they're not; I know there's heartbreak coming, but this morning my mood is up. Life's a bounce, a chase after a sprinter sun.

Alec's front field is in corn and beside the corn is a sign: *Sin, when it is finished, bringeth forth death.*

"*Life*, when it is finished bringeth forth death," I mutter, as Graham turns in at Alec's long lane.

Alec is in the barnyard, wielding a pitchfork. His hair in the sun is the same wavy brown as Graham's. Alec's father and our dad are brothers.

Graham and I get out of the truck and head for our cousin. In these parts nobody greets you or calls you by name. The approach is to sidle over to the person and make a few offhand remarks about the weather. Every now and then a quick glance in the direction of the other feller's face.

Graham mentions the hot sucker of a sun, then starts in on his troubles: "My car wouldn't start when I went to come up here this weekend, my tractor hitch is broken, the lawnmower died on the second row, the roof I got fixed last September is still leaking, Rosy cut herself on the barbed wire fence, and now Hell Bent is dead. My best gelding. Hung himself in Linda Blair's stable."

And your wife wants out, I add, silently.

Alec is leaning against the rail fence that encloses the barnyard, frowning at the black rubber toe of his boot. When Graham finally pauses, Alec looks up and smiles. The flasher sun has stopped and turned around, unbuttoned still; here in the barnyard, a short buzz from the manure pile, we three Kerrs receive the full frontal farce of his attentions.

"I have good news for you, Graham," says Alec.

"O-o-hhh? What's that?" says my brother, with the hint of a drawl that comes over him whenever he's with his kin.

"We will all be saved!" says Alec.

"O-o-hhh?" says my brother.

"All of us," Alec repeats. "Sinners, disbelievers, Catholics, horses, them that takes their own life – it don't matter to God. We will all be saved!"

City Woman

*A*gain this morning the beggar woman is in Lee's path. Right in front of the office building where Lee works in London, Ontario. As usual, the woman is standing with her legs far apart and she is rocking, rocking, rocking. Her hair is grey and straight. You could say she has a beard, so many long, black hairs are growing out of her chin. In the centre of her lips is a cigarette butt.

Lee used to know what to do when she saw a beggar in the street. Pass by without a qualm. Then she ran across something in the autobiography of a man she admired, a man of wisdom who was praising the woman he loved: "I never, ever saw her pass by a beggar without giving something." This sentence was to Lee like a jolt to a scrabble board, all the letters knocked out of their neat squares. Lee had been taught that it was wrong to give to beggars, that giving somehow caused more beggars.

The beggar woman's arms are straight out facing Lee, both hands encircling the tin can. Her eyes are the white-blue of a sky that shows itself in slivers between high city buildings, and the tail of her blouse flaps in the breeze like the torn poster on the hoarding Lee has just passed. Those pale eyes look right at Lee, and the woman moves the can to parallel Lee's steps.

Some mornings Lee looks back. Other mornings, like today, she averts her eyes and scuttles past into the insurance company. Lee has never put anything into the can.

In her twelfth floor office, Lee arranges and re-arranges the papers on her desk. She looks at her calendar and sees that today she lunches with Betty. Then, as she does every morning, Lee rests her chin in her hands and looks out over the office rooftops, lets her eyes slide into half-focus and rest on the moving clouds.

Lee is fifty-two years old. She does not leave her house to come to work until she is "all got up." That means work. Clairol copper hair washed and dried and curled and brushed and sprayed into the most flattering shape possible. Base, lipstick, blush, mascara, eye shadow artfully applied to her face. Nails filed and stroked with clear polish. Legs encased in run-free pantyhose of a shade to complement her outfit. Deodorant. That is the immediate effort. Then there is the background labour – visits to the hairdresser for perms and cuts and dyeing; shaving of her legs and armpits; plucking of chin and eyebrows; exercising of her stomach muscles; avoidance of food high in calories, that is, almost everything that tastes good.

All this so that Lee will have a natural, healthy, youngish look to her when she steps out her front door. All this labour and artifice to avoid looking like what she is – a woman who has lived half a century. The other day when she turned her eyes away from the morning clouds and the pigeons, she discovered a rogue thought sitting right on the surface of her mind like a woodchuck at the mouth of its burrow: *Maybe it's time to give it all up.*

Immediately into her mind had flashed an image of herself – how she would look if she gave it all up – being introduced by her husband Bruce to his colleague, Ron. Ron and his new young woman.

Several weeks ago now, her husband had opened his briefcase to remove a file, and Lee had seen a book lying there on top of the papers: *Get Your Tongue Out of My Mouth, I'm Kissing You Goodbye.*

"Is that Ron's book?" Lee had asked. Ron, like Lee and Bruce, is in his early fifties; he has just left his wife for a woman fifteen years his junior. Ron has recently taken to inviting Bruce for a drink on some of the evenings that his new woman friend is teaching yoga.

"No."

Lee picked up the book and turned it over, saw the public library label. "Did Ron take this out of the library and lend it to you?"

"Yeah, what is this anyway? The inquisition?"

"When I asked if it was Ron's book, why didn't you tell me?" questioned Lee, keeping her voice even and free of emotion.

"It's not Ron's book. What have you got against Ron, anyway?" Bruce retorted angrily.

Then, four weeks ago, Lee made another discovery.

Bruce had been doing his own laundry for years. On this Saturday morning, Lee noticed his basket overflowing with dirty clothes. In a surge of goodwill, she did three loads of laundry for her husband, folded and put it away. In Bruce's sock drawer, she noticed a white corner. Another book. She pawed away the socks. *Hot and Bothered: Men, Women and Sex in the Nineties.* Goose bumps had stood out like hives on Lee's arms as she slowly buried the book and closed the drawer.

At lunchtime, Betty's voice is scraping over stones. That's how Lee thinks of it. Betty's voice seems to be at the bottom of a gravel pit, scraping over sharp white-grey stones. Lee finds herself taking deep breaths as if she could float Betty's voice out of the pit, make it round and buoyant and full of possibilities.

Lee and Betty are outside the back entrance of the office where both of them work. Betty would have plunked her lunch on a table inside, but Lee suggested they sit on their sweaters under a maple tree. She wants to escape her temperature-controlled building where not a window can be opened. Lately Lee has the feeling that being confined inside day after day is subtly warping her.

Gulls teeter on the nearby garbage pails and launch into raucous flurries over spilled food. A saucy flapper of an east wind from Lake Ontario lifts Betty's hair into a crest. Lee sees that Betty will soon be one of those women whose scalp glints through her hair, no matter how she arranges it.

Betty is telling Lee the most recent instalment of the Betty-leaves-her-husband story. As Lee listens, she stares at Betty's lunch. Nachos curling under a thick cheese sauce, the orange of highway markers under a hot sun. White plastic fork and knife. A tomato hamburger mixture sloshing next to shredded lettuce strips slowly submerging in a creamy white sauce. Betty is as white as a Pillsbury dough man's baking cap. Her cheeks are puffy like floury tea biscuits, her stomach is a mounded loaf of bread under her striped taupe and white skirt. From Betty's sandal protrudes a toenail that is at odds with this lumpy whiteness. The toenail is tough and curved and sharp.

"Even though I've acted with so much 'courage' and all . . ." Betty is saying now. On the word 'courage,' Betty's eyes roll. Her head dips and for an instant her neck stretches horizontal, like a goose in flight. Others might call me courageous, say Betty's eyes and neck, others *have* said it, but I would never say it of myself.

"So I give myself a little talk," says Betty, her voice for a moment rising above the gravel. "Betty, you thought this out for years, you acted, well, *others* say you acted with 'maturity' and 'grace.' You'd worked hard on yourself, you'd arrived at the place where you deserved better. This is what you wanted. Your own apartment, all fixed up the way you wanted it."

Lee has visited Betty's new apartment, nine stories up in a highrise. She was invited along with two other women from Betty's support group. Lee had not realized she was part of any such thing until introduced by Betty to the other two women: "This is Lee, another member of my 'support group.'"

Betty had taken them on a tour. Rectangular rooms. As they toured, Lee had pictured the stacks of identical apartments in this building. Everything matching. The purple in the rugs and cushions picked up by the purple in the drapes. Lee had the feeling she was in the Home Furnishings department of Eaton's, the feeling she'd seen these rooms a thousand times.

"I splurged," Betty said. "I hired a decorator. My problem is I'm never sure what will look good. It was worth it to me to get professional help."

There was in Betty's apartment no clutter, no books, plants, newspapers, magazines, or CD's, no evidence of life that Lee could see. As she followed Betty and the other two women from room to room, Lee thought of her garden with its clash of colours and scents, its tangles of vines and plants. There were always more weeds than Lee could cope with, the garden always verging on chaos. Right now she wanted to be there, on her knees in the dirt, pulling weeds from between the flat stones and among the herbs. This tour was making her long for sweat, itches, leg cramps, soil beneath her nails, mosquitoes biting her temple.

After admiring the neat contents of the closets, the women returned to the living room. Lee's easy chair was positioned so far from the purple flowered sofa that she felt as if she were on one side of a stadium, the women on the sofa on the other side of the stadium. Betty coming and going with colourful plates of hors d'oeuvres was the performer for whom it was their job to root. How did I get this job, thought Lee. I don't want it. An immediate twist of shame then made her effusive in her praise of the celery curls and the radish roses.

Today Betty is stretching her neck and rolling her eyes for the second time. "Tom is seeing a woman," she says. "If you can believe *that!*"

The theme of previous lunches has been Tom's inability to cope. Lee has never met Tom, only formed a picture of him from listening to Betty. Tom never believed Betty would leave him, although Betty warned him many times what would happen if he did not change. He is unable to re-arrange the furniture after Betty takes half of it, unable to invite friends over (he has no friends), unable to know what to do with his weekends, unable to cope with the financial details of the separation.

Tom is Betty's audience, Lee has decided; he expresses dismay and disbelief at each new step Betty takes. Betty sees herself as the competent one. She describes Tom as a mother would describe a child she is weaning from her breast. At a previous lunch, Lee had asked Betty whether Tom might take up with another woman. "Oh there's no question of that," Betty had responded quickly. "He's dysfunctional."

"Dysfunctional?"

"Oh, you know, not interested in sex. He's . . . I think he's sexually dysfunctional."

"Would you be upset if he did find another woman?"

"There's no question of that. He's completely passive."

"Tom is seeing a woman?" Lee asks now.

"Yes, if you can believe it. I think she asked him out. They've been to the symphony and out to dinner. Somebody from work." Betty is stirring the shredded lettuce round and round with her plastic knife.

"How do you know?"

"Jill. She phoned me from Thunder Bay, like she does once a week, and the first thing she said was – did I know Dad was seeing another woman?"

"Have you told Tom you know?"

"I mentioned it casually. He was defensive, wanted to know how I'd found out." Betty reaches up and smoothes her hair, again raised and disheveled by the wind. "I have no right to be upset, but I am. I'm actually jealous." Betty scrunches her napkin in her fist and looks straight at Lee. "To tell you the truth, it's all I can think about."

Lee has the impression that trapped beneath the gravel of Betty's voice is a tightly confined torrent of water. She looks into Betty's eyes. She knows what her role is, but as always during these lunches with Betty, Lee feels as if she's pulling taffy with every movement, as if the day is enormously humid and she needs all her strength just to get through the ordinary motions of living.

"I can imagine how you must feel," she manages to say, as she gathers the paper plates and plastic cutlery for the garbage. "I'll see you later, Betty. I have to go round by the pharmacy."

As she hurries through the deteriorating mall, Lee imagines opening a drop-in centre in one of the many empty stores. Posting qualifications.

To be admitted, you must meet the following requirements: Alone. Always alone. Thin arms and legs. A hump on the back of your neck. Loose skin. Scalp glinting through your hair. Your belly as round and as full as once were your breasts. Your breasts as flat and as low as once was your belly. An air of Kresge's lunches about you.

Children and husband are protection from this, thinks Lee. So are all those things Lee does to make herself presentable before she leaves her house. You're not supposed to say that out loud anymore, but it's true. Calcium supplements are protection. And exercise.

A job. Above all, a job. Lee knows that her own job is not secure. Her company has already laid off people who thought they would be there for life.

At five, when Lee leaves work, the beggar woman is still there. Feet wide apart. Rocking, rocking, rocking. What does it mean? Betty's goose neck stretch and her eye rolling are ways of undermining herself. What is the beggar woman saying with her rocking? As Lee hurries past and jaywalks across the street to her parking lot, she pictures how she would look if she let herself go for even a couple of months – hair straight and white, dark sprigs of beard and moustache, hairy legs, scraggly eyebrows, blemished skin. Would the people she works with even recognize her?

Later that evening, she carries her supper to the patio. Again this week, Bruce is away on business. Pots of lemon balm, basil, and rosemary are at her feet. The air smells of lavender and old roses. Dark blue delphiniums bend and sway at odd angles just this side of the cedar hedge.

As she eats her strawberries, Lee reflects on husbands. There is something wrong with all of them. Her friend Debbie's husband will spend any amount of money that is in his pocket. Debbie confiscates his paycheque and doles out money in small amounts. Joan's husband does nothing in the evenings but watch TV, falls asleep in front of the set most nights. Another friend's husband is never home, between work and his passion for golf and tennis. Lee's neighbour's husband is too nice. All his spare time goes to helping friends move, fixing their broken appliances, helping them put on additions.

Betty's husband is not a wife-beater or a womanizer. Betty's husband's faults are in the above category. That's what Lee thinks. Once, these failings were considered part and parcel of being a human being, to be tolerated as a couple lived out their lives. Now women are leaving their husbands because of these failings. Are there lives really any better for so doing?

Lee gets up and pours her cold tea on the lemon balm. She untwists the hose and reaches through Virginia creeper to turn on the tap at the side of the house. She directs the cold spray onto the red and white impatiens and into her mind come the exchanges with Bruce that she manages to keep at bay all day. As she squeezes the hose handle harder, water courses onto the white impatiens like rain from a barn spout.

Now is the time her questions file by, stark as prisoners released from a dark place. Is Bruce going to leave her? Should she be leaving Bruce? If she does, or he does, will she end up like Betty in her high rise, or the invisible women in the mall, or the beggar woman? Or Minny her cat, fat and stupefied in a hot, sunny corner. How much longer can she tolerate life in her airless office?

Lee turns off the hose and returns to the twilit patio. The first fireflies are here, their light intermittent. From behind her, white nicotiana releases its haunting fragrance. She inhales the soft sharp scent of wet lavender and remembers a pair of small white gloves with pearl buttons she wore to Sunday school as a child. That bright, orderly time. How swiftly a world can disappear.

In the side yard under the weeping Nootka cypress, the light is dark blue. Beneath the drooping limbs of the cypress, Lee sees the beggar woman in her mind's eye. Rocking.

Suddenly she knows what it is, this rocking. A need for comfort. *Comfort me. I have no one to comfort me.* Why has Lee been so afraid of the beggar? She pictures herself, like the woman in the book, putting money into the beggar woman's can.

And now as the dark blue light leaves the garden, Lee also sees the weeping Nootka as a city woman, a tall woman clothed in wide-sleeved, flowing robes, standing with her arms upraised on this middle ground of the garden, the place where earth touches heaven. Lee is surprised to feel tears gently sting the back of her eyes as her heart forms a kind of prayer to the tree woman.

Oh, bless us with your weeping. Gather us in. Comfort and keep us all.

The Change

*M*aven Chesley is on her way to see a psychiatrist. In preparation, she has shaved her legs and changed the colour of her nail polish from intense fuchsia to shell-pink glaze. Last week, Maven's teenaged son said that his mother had a man's legs. He meant they were so hairy. Now they are smooth and partly hidden by a pair of new pantyhose. Spice-brown.

Maven's appointment is at nine a.m. She had her choice of nine or ten or eleven, and she chose nine. Might as well get it over with. Have something left of the day. She has allowed herself half an hour to get to the hospital. Partway there, she realizes she'll be too early. She stops her car in a No Parking space in front of a highrise apartment building. A man comes out of the building. He folds his bare, muscular arms in front of his chest. He plants his feet well apart. Maven decides she can wait just as well in the hospital parking lot.

It said "No Parking," not "No Stopping," she says to her rear view mirror as she pulls away.

In the hospital parking lot, she touches up her shell-pink lipstick and pats her short brown curls. Considering she's fifty, she doesn't look bad. This is a psychiatric hospital, not a regular hospital with a psychiatric unit. That means everybody here is crazy. Mad. Insane.

Retarded. Mentally ill. Mentally challenged. The other day, in a team meeting, one of the teachers described herself as height-challenged. Maven was sitting at the other end of the table. "Height-challenged?" she stage-whispered, "what the fuck happened to short?" Her end of the table broke up and Maven's boss gave her the look a teacher uses to impale the class troublemaker.

"You're gonna get yourself downsized right outta there," said Maven's husband George, when she told this story at supper.

"You said fuck in fronna those nerds you work with?" said Maven's teenaged son.

There are three patients on the front steps of the hospital. Maven can tell they're inmates. The way they're dressed. The way they look as if they have nothing better to do than stare at her. Their skin, lavatory white.

Twenty minutes ago when she left home, the sun was out. Now it's raining. She has no umbrella. If she walks from the parking lot to the hospital entrance with nothing covering her head, her hairdo will be ruined and right away she'll be at a disadvantage with the psychiatrist, shaved legs or not. If she dumps the apple cores and dirty Kleenexes out of the plastic bag on the floor of her car and puts the plastic bag over her head, her hairdo will be saved, but she'll look like an inmate.

From the parking lot, the hospital looks to be made of long, thin sections shooting off in different directions, like tentacles that have received an electric shock. The main entrance is at the hub of the tentacles. Better to look like a loony than to have her hair collapse, she decides.

"Nice hat," says one of the loonys as she approaches the front steps.

"Nice legs," says the second loony, gesturing with his cigarette.

The third stares at her in silence.

In the entrance lobby, Maven whips the bag off her head and fluffs her hair. "Could you direct me to the Mood Disorders Clinic," she says, to the person beneath the Information sign.

"Down the long hall to the very end and then right," says the young woman. "Brockton Psychiatric Hospital," she says into her mouthpiece. "Can I help you?"

Yesterday, when Maven stopped in front of the butcher shop to pick up her pork chops, there was a man sitting on the sidewalk. "Even BPH won't take me," he said, as Maven stepped around him to enter the store.

To help ensure that BPH won't take her, Maven has worn her best suit, a fine weave in antique gold. She enjoys wearing the colours of the season she's in. She has worn her spice toned pumps. She is the only person in this long thin hall. Her shoes go clok clok clok clok. Anyone watching would probably think she was staff.

Mood Disorders. Mood. I'm in a good mood. Are you in a bad mood today?

In. In a good mood. As if a mood were a container and you were inside it.

Mood. "The milking machine prong is pinching my teat," mood the cow to the farmer's daughter.

A mood seems to Maven a thing not-too-serious. A thing you could crawl out of if you wanted to.

She turns right. MOOD DISORDERS CLINIC reads the sign.

"I have an appointment at nine a.m. with a Dr. Kliapis," says Maven to the receptionist. Her watch says 8:57.

"Dr. Kliapis called. He'll be in before too long. Could you fill out this form, please."

Maven had thought it strange that the doctor had three appointments open only two weeks ago. She thought waiting lists for shrinks were months long. Now the doc is late. These are not good signs.

The receptionist looks not much older than Maven's teenaged son. The girl has three voices. The phone voice is richer, rounder, louder and nicer than the other two. The voice for the co-worker who is coming and going with papers is casual, flippant, even boastful. Then there is the one for the patient – for her, Maven, the loony. This voice is official and is lined with the feeling Maven had when she passed the three loonys on the front steps.

A stout little man clutching muffin-to-go zooms by the waiting room. "Morning," he calls to the receptionist, not slowing. One of the doctors, thinks Maven. He's late, for starters. And he's so short he'd have to become a shrink to compensate.

"You're just like this guy in my class," Maven's son had told her a few days ago. "You have Attitude."

"What's Attitude?"

"Attitude is when you expect the worst o' some nerd before you even meet him," said her son.

The stout little man hurries into the room trailing muffin crumbs. "Good morning," he says, offering Maven his hand, "I'm Dr. Kliapis. Sorry to be late. Come this way, please." Maven figures she has about ten years on this doctor, but his brown hair is streaked with silver and recedes from his forehead, giving him a tall face. Huge sapphire eyes almost take up the top half of this face. He looks as if he just stepped out of a UFO, thinks Maven. She catches a whiff of shaving cream. Or is it male perfume?

Dr. Kliapis' office is a fair distance down a different hall. The doctor moves so fast that Maven has to hurry to keep up with him. But then, wouldn't it be awkward if they walked side by side. Clok clok clok clok. It's a rainy morning, isn't it. Yes, it is rainy, isn't it. Clok clok clok clok. It's been a rainy fall, hasn't it. Yes it certainly has, hasn't it. Better to run so fast the patient stays behind you.

The doctor's office is so different from the rest of the hospital that it's like stepping from a bus station into a library. The walls are a silver-grey, the carpet is cream. Books fill the wooden shelves. Dr. Kliapis switches on a lamp with a cream shade, and a circular glow is cast just where the two of them will sit. The doctor closes his door and sits down across from Maven.

"Now," he says, leaning forward. "Why are you here? Tell me your story in your own words. Take all the time you need to tell me what's wrong."

There is a speech Maven wants to make to this doctor. She wants to turn his office into an auditorium, go before the lectern, lean into the microphone, fasten her eyes on her audience of one and spit her words hot and unforgettable into his space.

What's wrong? First off, I want you to know there's nothing wrong. With me. What's wrong is that other people think there's something wrong with me. Okay. I've always been a person who believes in calling a spade a spade. But almost everybody else lies.

Okay. Let me tell you why I'm here.

I'm fifty years old. Haven't had my period in four years. The change. That's what my grandmother called it. The change of life. Never mind menopause, let's call it what it is.

The Change

It's a change alright. You lose your looks, you lose your sex drive, sometimes you lose your husband. You lose your children to the world, you lose your ability to have more children. You lose your parents, you lose everyone in that generation. The ones who stood between you and death. You lose the thickness of your hair, the resilience of your skin, the cycle that's been containing you since you were twelve, and you lose the ability to focus on anything up close, including your ever more hairy chin. You lose either your figure or everything that's good to eat, you lose your protection from heart disease, you lose the juiciness of your private parts and if you are the one in nine, you lose a breast.

And what do you gain, doctor? You gain attacks that begin with a ten second hot flash of acute anxiety, then detonate a blast from hell in your veins. Attacks that repeatedly interrupt your sleep and soak your clothes, night and day. You gain weight, facial hair, thinning bones and invisibility to the opposite sex. And what do They say about the change of life? They say: "If you have a job, if you are busy and well-adjusted, you may find that you are through the menopause without even noticing it. One day you no longer have the fuss and bother of menstrual periods. What a pleasant surprise."

Well, Dr. Kliapis, I have a job and I am busy, but believe me, I noticed the change of life. I noticed that it took me longer and longer to keep myself looking like the youngish, pleasant Maven other people were used to seeing. The workload was incredible. Tweezing, plucking, dieting, dyeing, creams, perms, makeup, exercising. On and on and on.

So, one day last spring, I made a decision. I decided to go away for the summer to a deserted farm my cousin owns. Decided that for the whole summer, I would let myself go. Stop the upkeep. Just let myself look the way I'd look if I didn't do any of that stuff. I wanted to see, really see, what kind of creature The Change was turning me into.

Maven does not deliver this speech for her tongue cannot quite reach it. Instead she tells Dr. Kliapis the story of her summer . . .

It is late August. All morning she has been scything in the side yard that stretches across to the swamp. She enters the dark, cool porch, walks across the cement floor and opens the door to the back kitchen.

She picks up the tin dipper and fills it from the pail of well water. She drinks all of the cold liquid, then goes back outside to gather tomatoes and corn.

She has been here on the farm for ten weeks.

The hair on her head has been clipped short by her own scissors. It is white. Her brows have grown together. She has a white goatee, a dark, thin moustache. Her belly is round, her long breasts hang low, reminding her of the she-wolf who nursed Romulus and Remus. Her legs are covered with black hairs. Her toenails curl around the ends of her toes, thick and yellowish and horny. An animal's claws.

Mornings, she looks at herself in the mirror before she gets dressed. She does not look like a woman. She does not look like a man. The androgynous being who looks back from the mirror is sending double signals. The creature is unsettling, almost frightening, even to her. She has been right to seclude herself. But increasingly there is a familiarity; something recognizable is emerging from her unaltered physical self, as in the darkroom when an image gradually emerges from the chemical bath.

One morning, she gets it. She looks like a goat. She searches the short white hairs of her head for horns. There are none. That morning, she sets the timer of her camera, turns it vertically and stands before it for a self-portrait.

On a day late in August, she sits at the kitchen table for her lunch of tomatoes and corn and harvest apples. A little breeze carries the scent of phlox through the screened window. When she has finished eating, she carries her tea outside to the wooden bench that sags against the back porch. Flies make buzzing parabolas in the humid air and light on her bare arm and on the screen door.

Even without the mirror, she feels transformed. She cannot finger her beard and her moustache day after day and feel like a woman. She cannot feel her long breasts swing against her navel as she scythes and feel like a man.

She knows that in other times, other places, she would have been a god. She would have been worshipped for her brown face and her white beard. She would have breathed through her ears, her intermittently burning skin lit with an on-again, off-again glow. Her hand would have possessed a thong for the ritual fertility whipping of the women in the crowds who put themselves in her way to receive the fertility magic. On her feet, hooves.

In those days, the highest peak would have been her home. From it she would have seen all – past, present and future – her gaze the gaze of Christ. She, Maven. Damned. Saved. Lewd. Monastic. Simple. All Knowing. She, Maven, containing male and female, light and dark, good and evil.

She tosses the dregs of her tea on the shrivelled August rhubarb leaves. Her husband and son will be coming for her soon. Later today she will remove the hair from her face.

It is early evening. Maven is leaning into the small, back kitchen mirror shaving her goatee.

She has lathered the area with ivory soap (she does not use aftershave for she does not want to smell like a man) and has made her first three strokes with the straight blue disposable razor. These strokes catch and falter in the thick growth. She persists. She scrapes and scrapes until the goatee is gone and the newly naked skin puffy and red. With tiny scissors she clips the sparse dark hairs of her moustache. She opens the box of Silken Soft that will transform her hair to medium brown, mixes the product, and rubs it into her short curls. As she waits twenty minutes for the dye to do its work, she cuts her toenails short and paints them fuchsia. Upstairs, in her bedroom, the outside of her screen is dark with flies. She dresses in the navy shorts and top she wore the day she arrived here. Her bra feels like a harness.

When she is finished, she returns to the back kitchen and steps out into the twilight. She follows the path to the row of old pines that line the rail fence, the pines that never cease to whisper and creak and sigh. As she has done every evening all summer long, she climbs onto one of the lower bows, then steps up to her perch on a branch heavy with pine needles. There, all summer, she has rocked and dreamed waking dreams, wondering why nature has allowed her to live beyond her fertility, wondering what is left for her now. Her fingers have become black and sticky from the resin that oozes from the bark, just as they did when she was a young girl staying on this farm with her cousin. Tonight she protects her fingers with the pale blue gloves she wears to wash the dishes.

And tonight, as dusk settles beneath the pines, there is the sound of a motor, a car gearing down for the last hill before the lane curves towards the house. It is her husband and her son, come to take her home.

Her mouth is dry. For two hours she has been telling her story to this silent doctor. "My husband and son were appalled by the photograph I took of myself near the end of my stay. They think I have a dreaded disease, that at any moment I could relapse and become the creature of the photograph. I came here to appease them. They won't leave me alone about it."

Still the doctor is silent, looking at her with his brilliant eyes.

"Yes," he says finally, so softly she can hardly hear him, "yes, I've spoken with your family. Actually, I've seen the photograph." He leafs through her file, then closes it and leans forward. "There are many things we can do to help you, Maven. But I think it best that you stay with us for a while."

The doctor stands and smiles, opens his office door and gently motions Maven through. "Come with me," he says.

One of the Seven Signs

*C*hatelaine's cover story is on skin cancer. A poignant account of a young mother who had a third-stage melanoma removed from her back. Two years later she is dead, leaving behind Sarah, three, and Jason, five.

Beware of any jagged mole, says the article. Any mole that is larger than usual. Have it checked out by a professional.

Under her forest-green summer dress, which is patterned by tiny ferns and fronds in a lighter apple-green, Marya is wearing knee-high stockings. She replaces the magazine in the table, then slides her left knee-high down to her ankle and twists her leg so that she can see the mole on her left calf.

The mole has been there since she was born. It is large and jagged. Perhaps larger and more jagged than it used to be.

Goose bumps prick the skin on Marya's arms and legs as her imagination unrolls in one quick, lurid tapestry her own sad decline and premature exit from this world. Left behind, motherless, is the new love of her life. Tatiana.

At the time she becomes aware of her mole in a new way, Marya is thirty-seven and the mother of a two-year-old girl.

Marya and Joel have not had children automatically, as many people do. With a fountain pen, Marya had made two lists on thick, cream stationery. Reasons For Having Children. Reasons For Not Having Children. What decided them finally, Marya tells her friend Carol, was looking at the question from the point of view of a lifetime already lived.

"How would I feel, I asked myself," she says to her friend on this July afternoon, her amber eyes alight, "if I got to the end of my life and I'd never done it. I realized I'd feel as if I hadn't really lived. The cons just evaporated."

"For Joel, too?" Carol asks, "Did the cons just evaporate for him?"

"Yes." Marya is nodding her head. "Joe realized that being a father was something he wanted to do before he dies."

This is not true. The decision was Marya's. Though she involved Joel in the list making, though the discussions were lengthy and frequent, Marya knew that Joel would go along with what she decided. Why is she not admitting this to her best friend? "Carol, Joe would have had children or not had children. I could have brought him round either way. That's the truth."

Carol sighs and shifts in Marya's rocking chair, gently lifting her baby daughter Breanne away from her breast and resting her upright against the wad of clean diaper that covers her shoulder.

"And you know what else?" Marya continues. "That bugs me. It bugs me that I know he'll always do that. What I really want is a man who'll decide in his own soul what's true for him on the important questions. A man with that kind of depth." Marya touches the topaz that rests in the hollow of her throat and smiles at her friend. "And yet, I want my own way, too. I'd have hated if Joe had said no, if he'd decided he didn't want children."

Carol nods and lays her palm against the fat sole of her new daughter. The baby hiccups softly and milk runs from her mouth onto the folded flannelette. "Marya, I'm so glad we're friends. Our talks are somehow so . . . I don't know. Real. I guess that's it."

Tati can be heard in her upstairs crib, and Marya goes to fetch her. Carol switches Breanne to her right breast and watches her friend's tall, elegant figure climb the gleaming stairs. Not for the first time, Carol thinks that the artist who created her friend Marya (and for sure Marya's creator was an artist) worked from a brown palette. Not the taupes and duns of a sparrow's plumage, but the old golds and polished spices of autumn. Even in a Canadian February, Marya's skin will be an even, golden tan, as if she had spent that coldest of months on simmering cinnamon sand under a cerulean sky. Marya wears her dark bronze hair short, elegant long wisps cut at her neck and in front of her ears.

Carol is a petite strawberry blonde. Freckled. Cute. Beside her elegant friend, she sometimes feels like a new-world chest of wallboard, knocked together to be sold at a discount store.

At the sight of Carol, Tati hides her face in her mother's neck. "Anyway," Carol continues, "how did we get from your mole worries onto the subject of why we had children? What I came to tell you is what Trix told me." Trix is Carol's cousin who lives across the country in Vancouver.

"Oh, do tell. I forgot Trix was visiting."

Carol leans forward and expertly rolls the sleeping Breanne into her small stroller. "Trix's best friend is Kathy; you know, I've told you about her before." Marya nods, handing Tati an arrowroot biscuit from the package she is holding.

"Well, Kathy lives in an old neighbourhood of Vancouver. Houses like ours, a bit rundown, but still nice. Kathy has two little girls, one in grade two, one in nursery school. The oldest is the one who plays the violin already. Remember?"

Marya nods, her little finger wandering the curves of Tati's bronze curls. The child has turned now, to watch Carol speak, her eyes solemn above the tan biscuit.

"One day at noon, Kathy went to pick up her kids from school. When she got back, her front door was unlocked. She knew she'd locked it, was positive she had. And she thought that was strange. Really strange." Carol is sitting on the edge of the rocker's curved wooden seat, her green eyes bright. She looks like an intelligent little elf, thinks Marya, feeling Tati slide from her knee. "So she didn't go in. She went to Trix's house. She called the police."

"She called the *police?*"

"Marya, the police went to Kathy's house and there was a man in there. Waiting for her. Various instruments of torture ready for her and the two little girls. Marya, can you imagine?"

"How could he get in? Why wouldn't he have locked the door?"

"Maybe he forgot. I don't know. Trix is just beside herself. It's all she could talk about. Both she and Kathy are thinking about moving out of the neighbourhood."

Marya leans forward and the topaz winks brightly. Tatiana has dumped all the arrowroots onto the polished floor and is sliding them back and forth like toy cars. "Carol, that's the kind of story I wouldn't usually believe. If I read it in the paper. I'd think some of the details were missing. Like, the man was the former husband, he had a key, he wanted revenge. That way, it's awful, but it makes its own kind of horrible sense."

Carol wraps her toes around the steel bar of the stroller's frame. "This is Trix who told me, Marya."

"I'm not doubting it. I'm just saying *usually* I would."

Marya is on her feet. There are tears in her eyes, Carol sees, with surprise. "It's . . . do you know how that *Chatelaine* article about the mole ended, Carol? It described a man, a doctor, actually, who was swimming in his backyard pool with his Down's Syndrome daughter, and she told him he had a funny spot on his back. He paid no attention. Every day, she kept pointing at it, until finally he did. It turned out to be a melanoma, caught in time. Do you know what he said?" Through her tears, Marya sees that the light is slanting now, across the room, as far as the blue chair. "He said now he understood why she was born. His Down's Syndrome daughter. As if she had no value in herself, Carol, as if she was born just to save him."

Carol nods and gives her friend a long hug. "Call me tomorrow, Marya. I have to be going now."

Marya and Joel's last restoration project before they became parents was the yard. They made a front garden of miniature trees and shrubs – red Japanese maple, corkscrew hazel, weeping contorted birch. They mulched with red gravel and installed a black lamp post with a bronze fixture. They made a curving path from sidewalk to front door. In back, a grape arbour.

Joel did the actual digging and hauling. Marya designed the garden and picked out the plants.

When they were finished, Marya realized it was too perfect. Too fashionable. She stood back and imagined stones. Expressive stones of differing shapes and sizes, stones with faces, shadows, pock marks, juttings, curves, stones that would express the spectrum of human emotion, like sculpture. Stones and green plants. Moss. Maybe a tiny pool. No trees.

She wants to start over.

She says this aloud to Joel. She talks to him about stones.

"What?" he says. *"What?"*

"Nothing, nothing. I was just fantasizing out loud."

The following month, Tatiana is born.

The baby's skin is the colour of a field of ripe wheat on an August evening. Though she is a new-born creature, she smells of the earth in mid-summer, the earth redolent of cut grass and sweet clover and drowsing bees. Fulfillment and satiety. How can a tiny baby anticipate the mature woman in this way?

Her breasts heavy, her blouses sopping with excess milk, Marya moves in an endless cycle of feeding, bathing, changing, dressing, and rocking her child. Without anyone having shown her how, she has become Mother. The baby is placid. Her daughter asleep on her chest, Marya rocks for hours in a kind of trance. She can barely remember her life as an interior designer; she could not deal with a client now to save her soul. This exquisite weight on her chest completes her. All day and all night she breathes essence of Tatiana. What man could compete with this?

"You threw clean towels into the wash and left the dirty ones on the rack."

Joel is at the bedroom door addressing her. It is seven-thirty in the morning. Joel has been sleeping downstairs on the couch since the baby's arrival.

"What?" Marya is on her back in a milk stupor, the baby asleep on her chest. She twists her neck the better to see her husband. Joel's half-wet underarm hairs are pointing at her like accusatory spikes.

She shrugs in a way that she hopes is maddening, though she is hampered by the baby asleep on top of her. "If you're going to put out clean towels and leave the dirty ones there, what do you think is going to happen? How was I to know which were dirty?"

"With the nose you have on you, I thought you'd sniff it out. All you can talk about is the smell of the baby."

"I quit my job yesterday."

Marya had planned to prepare a dinner of chicken and tiny new potatoes, to open a bottle of Riesling. Over dessert, she was going to tell Joel about babysitters, how they watched the soaps and yakked on the phone while your child developed a suppurating diaper rash. Suppurating. That word would be the clincher.

"How could you do a thing like that without discussing it with me?" Joel stabs for his armhole, the deepening trough between his brows an outraged third eye.

"Joe, I didn't. Calm down. I didn't quit. You made me mad, okay? Yelling at me about the towels first thing in the morning. I'm thinking about it. We'll talk about it tonight."

A few minutes later, she hears the garage door. Joel has left for work. Without breakfast. Without saying goodbye. Lying there, musing about her husband from inside the rhythm of the sleeping Tatiana, Marya comes across a cruel thought.

That Joel has served his purpose.

He has given her his seed.

Last summer, on vacation at the lake, she'd picked up stones. When she first saw them, they were glittering, mysterious, unique. But dry, they lost their charge, turned plain and ordinary. The lot of her plain, ordinary husband now is to hew wood, draw water, bring home the bacon so that she can exist in this trance of new love.

"For now, I am cow." That's what she should have said to Joe; that's what she really meant. I am cow, and nothing more. For now, don't expect to find in me the wife and the career woman you once knew. Okay? Not forever, for now.

II.

Marya is wearing a sweater and Tati has on a fuzzy yellow sweatshirt. The doctor's office is in a high-rise, air conditioned building and Marya feels like a jar of pickles on the chill metal shelf of a fridge. She's covered with shiver prickles. How do people work here all day?

Dr. Harper is lifting Tati from the table, three-year-old check up complete. As he sits down and turns to his notes, Marya pulls down her left knee-high and twists her leg in his direction.

"Is this anything I should be concerned about?"

It is not possible to tell from the casual tone of her voice that off and on for a year Marya has twisted her leg around at odd hours. She has studied it outdoors by the light of the sun, indoors by naked electric bulbs; she has been to the library, has copied down characteristics of malignant moles, carried them deep in her purse, searched her mole for telltale blues and reds, begun to see these colours sometimes, maybe, in certain lights. Scolded herself.

Without speaking, Dr. Harper motions her onto the table and picks up his light. She can tell that he's annoyed at her, slipping this extra question into Tati's appointment. "When did this appear?"

"I've had it all my life, but I think it might be changing."

"It's always been there? It's benign."

"But I think it's changing."

"I'll send you to a specialist, but only to allay your fears. This is a benign nevi." That trick of throwing in the technical term, thinks Marya. To make him sound authoritative.

Can she tell Dr. Harper the other thing? The image?

She has rehearsed what she wants to say, knowing it will sound stupid to a man like Dr. Harper, a man who lives in a world of bacon and egg breakfasts, of impermeable walls and tidy, waterproof roofs. Dr. Harper is all of a piece, she can tell; he's united by the conviction that flows almost visibly through his body and into the world through his resonant voice. Whereas she, Marya, feels parts of herself drawn off by whoever she's with; any room she inhabits has siren songs in the corners and at the windows.

What Marya can't bring herself to tell Dr. Harper is that she's been seeing an image, at odd times, in the eye of her mind. Intruding. Obsessing her, like the mole.

One day she drew it for Carol. Parallel black lines, crisscrossed to create small, even squares. "What's that?" she asked her friend.

Carol shrugged. "Beats me. Lines and squares? A railroad track, maybe?"

"Every little while I see it, Carol. I'll be showing a client to the door or sitting at a red light or dropping off to sleep and suddenly there it is, in my mind." She described to Carol a recent dinner at

Joel's parents – how the discarded netting of the ham arrested her eyes. The neat, criss-crossing squares resonated with significance. She picked up the netting, nibbled the last sticky remnants of meat, and furtively placed the cord deep in her purse with the paper on abnormal nevi where she could take it out at odd moments to stare.

"My purse smells faintly of ham, Carol. I'm calling myself names. Loony-tunes. Crazy as a bedbug."

Dr. Harper is handing her the name of a dermatologist. Dr. Gregory. "The receptionist will call you in about a week with the appointment," he tells her, with one mighty exhalation transforming his rubber glove into a balloon with five fingers for the delighted Tatiana.

Dr. Gregory is a smiling man with a huge, blond pompadour and a line down the middle of his forehead that seems to divide his head into two planes. "That's benign," he says, switching off his light. "If I took it off, just to allay your fears, you'd be left with a big scar on your leg."

"I don't mind scars," says Marya.

"But it's benign."

"But I think it might be changing, and I thought one of the seven signs of cancer was 'any change in a wart or mole.'"

"Not to worry," says Dr. Gregory, closing his folder, getting to his feet, and smiling kindly at Marya. "It's benign."

October. Two small pumpkins make plump companions on the sunny windowsill. At fifteen months and three years, Breanne and Tatiana have begun to play together. Fat legs wide apart, Breanne is reaching into a bottom cupboard. Carefully, she hands pots and cookie sheets and lids to Tati, who lines them up against the wall.

"I have something to tell you," says Marya, when she and Carol have settled themselves at the wooden table and begun to blow on spoonfuls of leek soup. "I'm having the mole off."

"But I thought both Dr. Harper and the dermatologist said it was benign."

"They did, Carol. But the mole used to be flat and now it's raised. It used to be a plain, dark brown and now I see colours sometimes. I swear I do." Marya lays down her spoon and her amber eyes deepen to bronze. "Carol, once I could have faced the thought of death, but now, with Tati. To leave her would be . . ." Marya shakes her head and looks at her daughter.

"*Death?* But what did the doctor, the specialist, actually say, Marya?"

"Carol, when the nurse showed me to his office, there were two chairs. They were side by side, facing the same way, and they were so close they were almost touching. I sat down in one of them. When Dr. Gregory came in, he sat in the other. Picture it Carol. I felt ridiculous. I sort of shunted my chair away, and you know what he did?"

"What?"

"He got up and dragged his chair exactly beside mine again. There we were, like two people in deck chairs on a ship, staring straight ahead at the sky and the sea."

Carol breaks off a piece of the rye bread and dips it in her soup. "That is weird, but it doesn't necessarily mean the guy is a bad doctor. Marya, I don't know if I should say this, but do you think something might be bothering you that's not really the mole?"

A series of shattering clangs cause both women to jump. The stack of pots has crashed, and both little girls look at their mothers. "Careful there," says Marya. She gets up to fetch coffee to the table as the children leave the pans and lug the two pumpkins into the hall.

"Carol, I'm having the mole off because of the story Trix told you a year ago about Kathy. About the man who was in her house, waiting for her."

"What do you mean?" Carol wraps her small hands around the warm cup, her green eyes on Marya's face.

Marya has left her coffee and is standing with her back to the window, facing Carol. "I've thought about that story and thought about it. It's haunted me. I knew you were kind of mad that day when I changed the subject, but I couldn't talk about it. It wasn't just that it was horrible. I was braiding Tati's hair a few days ago when I finally realized what's been bothering me."

"What is it?"

Marya sits back down in the chair nearest her friend and leans forward. "If I'd been in Kathy's situation, Tati and I would be dead, Carol. The man would have got us."

"Why?"

119

"Because when I came home and found my door unlocked I *wouldn't* have been sure I locked it. Even if I knew I had. I would've told myself I must be wrong. I wouldn't have trusted myself, Carol. I'd have been afraid of looking to the police like a silly, hysterical woman. I would have gone in."

Four days after the minor operation on her leg, Marya's phone rings. It is Dr. Harper himself. "The mole was dysplastic," he says.

"What's dysplastic?" asks Marya. She is holding the phone between her neck and chin. One hand holds her leg steady; with the other she is slowly and carefully peeling off the bandage on her calf.

"Dysplastic is halfway between normal and cancer. The mole had to come off, Marya." Dr. Harper's normally resonant voice has thin places in it, like the ozone layer.

Marya does not answer. Her amber eyes hold a fierce and tender light, for they gaze upon a prey that has been sought so long it has taken on the patina of a beloved. There on her calf where the mole has been is the image that has appeared to her so relentlessly over the past year: parallel, black, criss-crossing stitching forming neat, small squares.

The One I Love

*O*n the plane from Toronto to Houston, Alice replays in her mind the January telephone conversation with her best friend Rooey. Rooey had described the one hair on the mons pudendum of her eleven year old daughter; this was a few seconds into Alice's and Rooey's first conversation in two years. Rooey said she thought it was a dog hair in that unlikely spot till she tried to brush it off and discovered it was attached.

How like Rooey to jump immediately to the mons pudendum, thinks Alice, as she accepts a coffee from the flight attendant. How like Rooey to roll that word off her tongue like a greased navy bean. Most people begin with the big picture, the general, the outer, then edge tentatively towards the intimate, the particular, the inner. Not Rooey. Rooey jumps to the mons pudendum like a flea to the leg of an owner returning home after a month's vacation. Rooey never even sees the big picture.

Rooey lives in Houston, Texas now. She is Alice's best friend in the way that a mother is a Mother, holding the title because she was there from the beginning. Alice has seen Rooey seldom in the past thirteen years, not at all in the past five. She wonders if she even knows her best friend any more.

Rooey's real name is Ruth. That's what her parents called her. Her friends called her Ruthy. It was her husband, Johnny Arendia, who named her Rooey. Even though Alice has been friends with Rooey since they were both five, she too now calls her by Johnny's name.

"I'll have to clean up the house before you get here," Rooey says on the phone in January, as they plan for Alice to come to Houston during her March break from teaching English at Glenmorris High School in Toronto.

"What do you mean? Surely you don't think you have to clean up for *me!* I'm your oldest friend, remember?" Alice replies.

"It's the animals. We have a mouse and two rabbits now, you know, as well as the dog and the bird. And the fish."

"Are they all in the house?"

"Well, the dog and the rabbits are supposed to stay outside in the pens Johnny built for them, but they're in the house quite a bit." Rooey goes on to describe in detail how the mouse shit differs from the rabbit shit and the dog shit differs from the bird shit. This is long distance, thinks Alice, and I'm paying. She shakes her head. As ever, Rooey seeing only what is under her nose.

As Rooey's dissertation continues, Alice's mind wanders to a visit she made once to her friend's apartment in Toronto when Rooey was still single and in medical school. Rooey had two cats then; Alice could tell that even before she opened the door of the apartment. The next morning, Alice turned on the electric frying pan to make scrambled eggs. An odour she couldn't identify permeated the air. "Fried cat piss," said Rooey. "Yang likes to go in there. You have to wash the pan before you turn it on."

Rooey's tolerance so infinite that it extends even to the excretions of the creatures that enter her world.

Johnny Arendia is facing the luggage carousel in the Houston airport as Alice approaches behind him. Though she has not seen him for five years, she knows him at once. He is wearing a Stetson with a cock-of-the-walk tilt. This tilt is contradicted by the heels of his boots. Each is ground down to the sole along the outside, giving him the bowlegged stance of a man who could slowly break apart along the mid-line. Is this what is meant by down at heel, Alice wonders?

Johnny's blackish-grey hair is long enough to curl around his collar and lie there round and smooth, like the cardboard gut of a roll of toilet paper. The prow of a huge white moustache thrusts beyond his ear. It is the hair length and moustache of a man who is bald on top and needs to compensate with more hair in other places, a man who would like, but does not dare, to meet the world with fly unzipped, pubic bush still springing rich and full. Yet Johnny Arendia is not bald. His curly hair is not even thin on top.

"Hola!" says Alice, as she comes close to his back. It is all the Spanish she knows. Johnny whirls and hugs her; she receives a whiff of turmeric, an image of beans roiling black and turgid on a forgotten burner. *Double, double, toil and trouble* is what goes through her head. So often there is a fragment like this providing an unwanted undercurrent to Alice's thoughts, sometimes flowing under the surface of her day for hours, sometimes only for minutes. Johnny tells Alice they have an hour's drive on the expressway before they reach home. He picks up one of Alice's suitcases and leads her to the car.

Rooey was Alice's only friend all those years they were growing up. Alice always preferred that Rooey come across the street to her house to play. The paintings on the walls of Rooey's home were incomprehensible, the temperature was ten degrees colder than Alice was used to, and the cooking smells put Alice in mind of twisting alleys and doorless huts. Vibrating, penetrating voices wailed from the living room turntable, and Colin Steinberg, Rooey's father, said words like menstruation right in the middle of dinner.

Rooey's father had died five years ago. Alice remembers just how she felt when she heard the news that Colin Steinberg was dead. If a man like Colin could die, Alice realized – a man so learned and so in control, a man with an answer for every problem – then anyone could die. Socialist, omnivorous reader, benevolent king of the castle at home and at work. Alice remembers the fight she had with her best friend when Rooey said that her father had read the whole Bible. "That's impossible," said Alice. Alice's parents read Reader's Digest once a month.

"I did not marry Rooey because she is a doctor" are Johnny's first words to Alice on the expressway. I am not a crook is the fragment that enters Alice's mind. "I married Rooey because I love her," says Johnny Arendia. "I LOVE HER." Johnny's left arm steers the car, his right chops like Alice's Henckel knife at home in her kitchen in Toronto.

"I will tell you the truth. When I went to Rooey in Boston, she was living in an apartment. She had nothing. NOTHING." This time, the chopping arm narrowly misses Alice's nose. "She made thirty thousand dollars. We can buy NOTHING with this. Nothing . . . Rooey had nothing."

Each of his sentences is like a wave. The words crescendo, crash with a shout at the climax, and ebb. The ebb is delivered *sotto voce*, the thought of the climax seeping away in a whispered cadenza. "Nothing . . . Rooey had nothing."

Alice knows the events of Rooey's life. Alice was there, in Cuba, when Rooey met Johnny, but Johnny is telling her this as if she is a stranger.

"We moved to Kingston," he continues. "Rooey made eighty thousand dollars. We bought a beautiful house. BEAUTIFUL. Then the trouble started at work. Jealousy between the psychologists and the psychiatrists. Everybody resigns. Rooey is the LAST to resign . . . the last."

"I will tell you the truth. I love Rooey. But Rooey is a person who does not know how things work, how things are. Rooey is a stupid person. Not stupid. How do you say? Silly? No." Johnny twists in his seat. "Listen to me. If you will come to Cuba with me, you will expect me to know where to live. You will expect me to know *how things are*." Johnny takes his eyes off the road and keeps them on Alice's face until she nods.

The car has been losing speed with each paragraph of Johnny's story. They are in the middle lane. Drivers are passing on both sides, looking at Johnny as they zip by. It is midnight. The plane was delayed for hours. Alice had thought she would roll back the seat and rest for this last lap of her journey to Rooey's. She takes a deep breath and contracts her stomach muscles as tightly as she can. No matter what is happening, Alice does this every four hours, on the hour. She never misses. Her stomach is as flat as the plains of Texas.

Johnny is silent as he changes lanes in preparation for exiting the expressway. Alice sees herself hanging up the phone after that January phone conversation with Rooey, then looking outside at the sun on the ice-coated telephone wires. The cold has penetrated the brick walls of Alice's house this winter of her forty-second year, even reaching Alice in her rocking chair by the register. The snow is up to her window sills, the evenings so quiet. Alice used to like her white carpet. But this winter, her eyes have sometimes lost focus, and the carpet has seemed to shift and take on the aspect of a frozen northern tundra. Alice thinks she should get to know her best friend again, even get to know Rooey's daughters. Alice's husband Tom is a civil servant, a computer expert. This winter, he's been more preoccupied than ever with his work.

"Rooey took a job in Saskatoon. CONJO!"

Alice jumps. The climax of this wave is like a blast from an M-60 machine gun.

The next time, Johnny's face is suddenly as close to Alice's as his arm. "You have been in Saskatoon?" Alice shakes her head.

"Conjo! It is cold. The opposite of here. Here you cannot go out for five months because it is so hot. There you cannot go out because it is so cold. Let me tell you something." The arm again slices hard through the enemy between them. "There I was always angry. I suffer very much. EVERYONE is a communist. Everyone." Johnny's eyes leave the road again. "Everyone."

"After five years there is again trouble with the job, and we come here." Now Johnny grasps the wheel with his chopping arm and rummages in the left door pocket. He pulls out a gun. The weapon hangs above them, sullen in the yellow murk of the street light.

"Here you cannot live without fear," he says.

Reminds me of the one I love deep in the heart of Texas goes the song in Alice's head as they pull into the driveway of her best friend's home in what looks to be a wealthy suburb. The house is in darkness; the rest of the family have given up waiting and gone to bed.

Alice awakens the next morning at nine-thirty in the spare bedroom. The house is still silent. She goes into the tiny adjoining bathroom. She brushes her waist-length, white-blond hair, braids it into one braid and winds it around her head like a crown. Alice has been wearing her hair like this for twenty years. She gets dressed in a pale blue pantsuit, then puts on foundation, blush, lipstick, eye shadow and mascara. Now she is ready to open the door. *They're changing guard at Buckingham Palace/Christopher Robin went down with Alice.*

Alice walks into the bright living room. No one is around. She knows Rooey must be already at work and the children at school, but where is Johnny Arendia?

She steps outside into an unfamiliar world. The woolly Chow dog. His name is Bear, Alice remembers, from her last conversation with Rooey. "Hi Bear," she says tentatively. The dog shows his blue tongue.

Pink azalea. A spindly tree with rough, rackety leaves. Two magpies flipping down to splash in the dog's water bowl. A mockingbird. There in the pen are the spotted brown and white rabbits – Violet and Percussion – their names scratched onto the metal of the pen's side.

Alice steps back inside and gives herself a tour of the house, omitting the bedrooms; she considers them private property. Every surface of the family room and kitchen of Rooey's house is heaped with the detritus of living. Alice enumerates what is visible on the coffee table: a flashlight, a can opener, slippers, crayons, an apple core, bills, magazines, a pair of child's underpants, socks, a garden glove with holes in the fingers, a stethoscope, used Kleenexes, a package of peanuts. This is only what Alice can see. Underneath are layers and layers more.

Alice feels that trembling in her solar plexus that comes over her when any item is out of place in her own house. She is unable to leave her home in the mornings until the bedrooms and kitchens are restored to perfect order, water marks polished from taps, toilet lids raised and checked for stains or hairs – although Alice does not allow the idea of stains or hairs into her mind even as her eyes search for them. What does Rooey's mother think when she comes here? Alice wonders. Rooey's childhood home had bristled with a formidable, even ostentatious lack of dirt and chaos.

Bear is barking on the patio. Johnny Arendia is coming through the gate and into the kitchen with a bag of groceries. "Come over here," he says to Alice, as he sets the bag on the table "I have something for you."

As Alice approaches, Johnny reaches into the bag and takes out a large pineapple. "I will cut it," he says.

He picks up a knife and makes four long strokes. Now Johnny motions again to Alice, points at the core. "You know what we say in Cuba?" His brown eyes are the colour of the hard little ovals Alice has noticed in the rabbit cage. "A pineapple is like a woman. The sweetest part is by the bumbo."

The bumbo, thinks Alice, as she picks up a piece of the pineapple. It is Rooey's bumbo that got her her husband.

Alice and Rooey were inseparable until University, and then Rooey got boyfriends. Nothing Alice couldn't tolerate, until Benjamin came along.

Ben Hirsch was blond and ambitious. He was crazy about Rooey, with her long curly hair and her easy ways. Alice could see that Ben intended to marry Rooey. Rooey was only twenty-one, and Alice knew that was too young to make such an important decision, so she took Rooey aside and had a talk with her. Rooey broke off with Ben. Alice had that kind of power over Rooey.

Rooey's next boyfriend, Jake, lived in a flat several blocks from the University. Rooey stayed over at his place for days on end. All the time she was going with Jake, her legs and arms were a strangely changing palette of lemons and mustards, slates and pewters, charcoals and olives. Alice didn't pay much attention. She had met Tom, the computer programmer who would soon become her husband.

Jake left Rooey for someone else and men gradually became scarce in Rooey's life. Alice felt that Rooey was letting herself go. Rooey's rear end became like two sofa cushions hurrying along behind her, each half with a mind of its own. One half quivering, like Jello, the other half oozing in and out like an inner tube losing its air.

Alice's body was so flat and so muscular it was like a washboard – you could've turned it sideways and scrubbed clothes on it. Alice didn't have children and didn't want them, but Rooey wanted them so badly that when she turned thirty-five and no husband was in sight, she told Alice that the only thing that stopped her from getting herself artificially inseminated was her strong belief that children need a father.

That February, Rooey and Alice and Tom went on a vacation to Cuba. Johnny Arendia was their tour guide.

"Rooey," he said, on the second day, "you have a monumental

bumbo." This was meant as a compliment and Rooey received it as such.

"How can she stand those eyes and those hands on her all the time?" Alice asked her husband on the third day.

"I think she likes it," answered Tom. "Rooey's not like you, you know."

Rooey and Johnny corresponded. A year later, Johnny, who was divorced, left Cuba in a small open boat. Less than ten months after he arrived in Boston, where Rooey was now practising psychiatry, Sarah was born. Emily followed three years later.

"I have a surprise for you," says Johnny now, as Alice finishes the third long, pale yellow section of pineapple and puts her dish in the crowded sink. He reaches into his shirt pocket and takes out a piece of paper.

Alice sits back down at the table to read the note. It is from Rooey. "Alice, I'm terribly sorry. The boss called yesterday when you'd already left. I have to go to Waco, as part of his research team. They've let a lot of traumatized people out of the compound, and we're going to be interviewing them. You know my specialty is post-traumatic stress disorder, and this thing is right on our doorstep. The chance of a lifetime. The girls are with my mother in Austin. Johnny will take you anywhere you want to go. I'm really, really sorry about this, but I have no choice. I'll phone you as soon as I can."

Alice feels herself get hot all over. She cannot believe what she has just read. Stay here alone with Johnny Arendia? Not see Rooey or her daughters? She's paid all this money to come down here against her better judgment, really, and now she's in a situation like this! She probably can't even reach Tom. He's at that government think-tank thing in Niagara Falls this week.

Alice gets up. Her legs feel funny. She wonders if they will carry her back to the spare bedroom.

On the dot of twelve, Alice does her stomach exercises, then decides to have lunch on the patio and try to think what to do. Eight, noon, four, eight – Alice prides herself that in the two years she has been doing these exercises, she has never once missed.

She takes the can opener from beside the underpants on the coffee table and holds it under hot water for two minutes to sterilize it, then opens a can of peaches and pours them into a bowl. She brings the kettle to a boil and makes herself a cup of tea, finally finding the cups in an odd cupboard over the fridge. *And the crack in the teacup opens/A lane to the land of the dead.* Out on the patio, she positions her chair so that her back is to the hedge of dark pink azalea. Its lushness distracts her. Alice rubs her hands. They are always cold, even on a warm day like today.

A few minutes later, the back door slams. Johnny Arendia is standing over Alice, his fingers making their choreographed swirl across his moustache. A sultry wind lifts his curly hair into a jagged cock's comb. "Let me tell you something," he begins.

"Always I wanted a brother. That was my dream. When I meet Rooey, I think her father will be like a brother with me."

Johnny sits down on the chipped iron chair and hitches it closer to Alice. "I love Rooey's father very much. I LOVE HIM. When he dies, I suffer very much. I cry. But let me tell you the truth. Rooey's father is a communist."

"Oh?"

"Oh YES!" Johnny is on his feet. He picks up the metal chair and strikes the patio bricks with it, then turns it backwards and sits on it again. He leans close to Alice. "Oh yes. A Communist."

"I will tell you what happens in Saskatoon when Rooey's mother and father come to visit. I have many discussions with Colin. This day, I see in the paper an article about the man the Russians keep in prison for ten years because he tells the truth. You know?" Alice nods. The leathery leaves of the banana tree make a sudden hollow tapping over her head. "I show this story in the newspaper to Colin. Finally I have the proof about Russia. Conjo! You know what he says to me?" Alice shakes her head. Johnny rises from the metal chair and bends close. Alice sees tiny black hairs growing in the pores of his nose. "He says, 'Johnny, don't believe everything you read in the newspaper.'"

Johnny sits back down, presses his face against the dusty surface of the patio table, and beats it with his fist. "Conjo! He makes me crazy."

Johnny springs to his feet and jumps back towards the barbecue, then starts towards Alice. There is a she-bear's loom to his head and shoulders. "I go over to Colin and I take his shirt in both my fists and I say, "You fucking. You fucking. You sonofabitch. You sonofabitch." Johnny leans close to Alice as he says this. Alice does not breathe. Is he going to take her blouse in his fists?

Johnny's face puckers and reddens. He sits back down. Tears pop from his eyes and beat into the dirty patio table like miniature mortar rounds. "You sonofabitch! Colin."

As he utters the name of Rooey's father, the harshness of his tone cracks unexpectedly into a tenor bleat, a lost note, utterly bereft. Bear hurries from the garage, stands on his hind legs and places his woolly head beside Johnny's. The dog whimpers against Johnny's ear. Johnny takes a dark, stained cloth from his pocket and blows his nose. He looks straight at Alice. "I feel like I can kill him," he says. "I feel like I can kill Rooey's father." Johnny puts his face so close to Alice's she can see the shreds of breakfast pineapple between his teeth. "I have been in Angola, you know."

"Oh my God," says Alice. The peaches are slithering like worms inside her. "Oh my God, what did Colin do?"

"He looks a little scared."

Now Alice sees Colin's face clearly. She sees another patio, the one in the backyard of Rooey's long ago family home in Toronto. Another spring. Lilac and mock orange. Forget-me-not and lily of the valley. She'd gone to that patio every evening after supper the May of her grade eleven year so that Colin could help her with her physics. Alice remembers one May evening so humid they'd been complaining they couldn't breathe. Colin was in a short-sleeved blue and white shirt. Alice was surprised when she saw his bare arms. Thin and round and white. Hairless. Like a young girl's. Like Rooey's.

Colin finished making the notations in Alice's notebook, then laid down his pencil and stretched. Alice saw the underside of his wrist. White and shy, like a frog's belly. Blue veins like old fashioned flowers on a white china plate.

"Rooey comes running." Johnny's voice is again crashing against Alice's ear. "'What's the matter? What's the matter? Johnny. Johnny. What's the matter?' She cries. Rooey cries VERY MUCH." Johnny shakes his head. "She cries very much."

He gets to his feet and blows his nose again, pauses with his hand on the back door knob. "I will tell you something," he finishes.

"I love Rooey. But her father makes me suffer VERY MUCH . . . very much."

Johnny Arendia turns and without a backward glance re-enters the house.

Alice puts the spoon back in the empty bowl. There is a red mark where it has cut into her hand. She looks around for Bear, wanting to put her hand on his woolly coat, and sees Rooey's bicycle leaning against the garage. She wheels it onto the road and mounts it unsteadily, begins to ride it up and down the straight, flat streets of the suburb.

The houses are all the same, the yards invisible behind fences. There is not a human being to be seen. As Alice pedals, she sees Colin, then Johnny. Two kings of the castle. Colin and Johnny, each a dirty rascal to the other. Put them in a mixing bowl and blend to get a whole man. Alice begins to feel that she is not quite here on the bike. She is somehow transparent, like limbs seen on an X-ray. Any slight gust from behind the junipers or the elms or the cypress that line these narrow corridors could blow right through her, blow her away. Her legs feel like dream legs, not able to propel her properly. *And the bicycle went slower and slower/Because of that back-pedal brake.* It is not until she has finally found her way back to Rooey's, replaced the bicycle beside the garage, and closed the bedroom door that she looks at her watch. Four o'clock has come and gone, and Alice has not done her stomach exercises.

Alice has changed out of her grease-stained pant-suit and into a white skirt and top. She is lying on the spare room bed. Can it be that this is still her first day in Houston? She has been trying to think what to do, but her thoughts are like bowling balls in a large empty room where the floor slopes on all sides towards the centre. They slam together and ricochet off the walls with hollow, booming cracks. Some of the thoughts are about Rooey, about Rooey at Waco, about babies beaten and children held hostage, about David Korash, the devil who thinks he's Christ. Among the thoughts, a rhyme thuds incessantly: *Colin is gone/And Johnny lives on. Colin is gone/And Johnny lives on.*

On the oak dresser in the corner is a picture of Rooey with Colin and Esther. Alice remembers the last time she saw Rooey at Colin's memorial service in Toronto.

"Johnny really loved my father," are Rooey's first words. "He's suffered so much since we got the news. He's cried and cried."

"What about you?" Alice asks.

"I can't believe he's dead," Rooey says. "What will we do without him?" She turns to smile at the next person in the line of mourners. Rooey's eyes are like seaweed in cloudy water.

There is a knock on the bedroom door. Alice starts and jumps off the bed.

She opens the door. There is Johnny Arendia. Johnny has showered and lacquered his hair and moustache with perfumed oil. He is wearing a tangerine shirt and black jeans. His shoes shine like the polished weapon that hung above them in the street light the night before.

Alice stares and clutches the knob. "Dinner is ready," he says.

Alice's legs still feel like dream legs as she follows Johnny down the hall. *Alice is marrying one of the guard/A soldier's life is terrible hard, says Alice.*

The Texas sun is disappearing behind the pecan trees at the edge of Rooey's property. A sultry wind lifts the petals from the azalea, rattles and flaps the long leaves of the banana tree. Alice steps onto the patio, and the wind whips her white skirt between her legs. For an instant she seems to hear Colin's escalating falsetto giggle, sees him sitting in the worn brown chair in his long ago living room, hands folded over his puff pastry of a tummy as he listens to his new *Beyond the Fringe* record: *Will this wind be so mighty/as to lay low the mountains/of the earth?*

Johnny Arendia is standing in the long shadows beside the barbecue. On the picnic table is a bottle of Sangre de Toro and two steaks. Blood seeps along the margin of the T-bone cross. Beside Johnny, a grease fire erupts on the barbecue. Alice moves towards the flames.

The Mountains Will Not Care

Dedicated to my long-time colleague, Karen Cooper

*T*he magazine she holds has front and back cover missing. An old issue of *Saturday Night* that has somehow escaped the garbage. The magazine contains an article on Glenn Gould by Robert Fulford, who was a boyhood friend of the pianist genius. Glenn Gould's mother was proud of her son, Susan reads, but exasperated by his habits. She was a part-time voice teacher, her husband an amateur violinist.

Fulford writes: "They weren't prepared . . . for the arrival in their midst of Glenn Gould: it was rather like having a mountain range appear suddenly in the backyard."

Susan reads this sentence three times. For some reason, it has great resonance for her.

"I guess you wouldn't mind me keeping this old thing?" she says to the smiling assistant who beckons her in to the dentist's office. "There's an article I'd like to finish."

The cavities turn out to be deeper than Dr. Morley had foreseen. Part-way through the drilling, he stops to inject more freezing. When at last she is released from the padded chair, her faculties feel as frozen as her face. The washroom mirror shows one nostril obscenely flared, the other insensate. One side of her mouth gives a grotesque twitch, the other is quiescent.

"You're a fine-looking parent to show up at school for an interview," she says aloud, experimentally, but her tongue is clumsy. Even her left eye is numb.

Magda's teacher, Mrs. Gordon, will think her a fool.

Though it is the last month of her daughter's grade three year, Susan has not met Mrs. Gordon for Susan is busy and Magda's school life seems almost charmed. Her daughter is a model student, a friend to all. At home, Magda behaves like a normal nine year old, except for the evening hour between eight and nine.

Trespassers Will Be Prosecuted reads the sign on the heavy door of the school's front entrance. *All Visitors (Including Parents) Report To The Office.* Then the never-forgotten smell of sweaty-grubby and pencil shavings.

Mrs. Gordon is waiting in the office. She is a tall, natural blonde of about thirty, careful eyebrows pencilled in place. "We're meeting with Mr. McFadden," she tells Susan, offering her hand, which is as damp as Susan's is cold. "The Principal," she adds, unnecessarily.

Mr. McFadden is small and bald, dry and crisp. When they are seated and Susan has attempted a joke about her frozen face and awkward speech, Mrs. Gordon hands her two sheets of foolscap.

"Have you seen this before?" she asks.

The sheets are covered with Magda's neat printing. Susan looks from Mrs. Gordon to Mr. McFadden. She shakes her head. "What is it? A composition?" she asks, stupidly, hearing her unresponsive tongue fail to deliver clearly the word composition.

"The composition was supposed to be true," says Mrs. Gordon. "We talked about that for a week before the children wrote it. The best composition is to be entered in a city-wide contest. There's money involved. If it's not true, it's like an athlete winning because he took drugs."

"Magda is a highly intelligent child, Mrs. Johnston, and her composition is by far the best," says Mr. McFadden. "That's why we're taking this very seriously. There is no doubt she understood that the story was to be true." He looks at Mrs. Gordon, who nods. "This is cheating, plain and simple," adds Mr. McFadden.

"Not only that," says Mrs. Gordon, "Magda continues to insist that the story is true."

She is in a courtroom, or a trap. That much is clear to Susan Johnston. Bowing her head over her child's printing, she begins to read.

With the first sentence, the office vanishes, and she is on the western plains. It is summer.

✼

There is a subliminal listening even in Magda's luminous sea blue eyes. When she is six, a team of medical assistants comes to her school to test hearing. Her class is tested at the end of the day. Magda sits as still as a mannequin while the large earphones are placed on her straight black hair. She listens, then tells what she hears.

Rustling and cracking, the assistant kneels and leans close, blasting the little girl with her astonished coffee breath. "Sweetheart," she says. "You have the most acute hearing in the whole school."

"Cute?"

A fan of creases appears suddenly between the nurse's brown eyes and her ears. Another flurry of rustling and cracking. "Acute. Keen. You have the best hearing in the whole school, Magda. By far."

A week later, there is a white envelope in the letter box. Susan Johnston's eyebrows disappear beneath her thick, salt and pepper bangs as she reads about the results of the hearing test. But she says nothing. It is Magda's grandmother who talks to the little girl when Magda goes for her summer visit to the country, so far north that even in August the nights are cold.

Magda usually watches the eyes when a person is talking to her. But her grandmother has tiny black hairs growing out of her nose, and it is these hairs Magda watches, these hairs that give her the clues.

Her grandmother is big and round-shouldered, like the mother bear Magda once saw on a class trip to the Toronto Zoo. Her grandmother has long braids made of black and white hair twisted together. She moves slowly from wood stove to table, preparing their breakfast of fried trout. Each morning, it is Magda's job to drag the bread through the drippings left in the pan. Then she and her grandmother sit down to eat the fresh fish and warm, greasy bread. This mixture sometimes overflows Magda's mouth; she can feel it dripping contentedly from her chin. Her grandmother looks on. "Thy mouth runneth over," she says one morning, with a smile that begins in the tiny black hairs.

One day, Magda notices that her grandmother's nose hairs are small soldiers about to salute. "God has given you special hearing," her grandmother says that evening, after a supper of corn on the cob and apple-sauce. "And there is a reason."

Magda waits until it seems that her grandmother has nothing more to say. "What is the reason?"

"When God is ready, He will tell you. Stay alert. If you are listening in the right way, you will hear." Magda's grandmother kneels and now she is the same height as Magda. There are thin black hairs above her lips. Among the hairs are dewdrops, and straight up and down lines. Grandmother stretches out her fingers and traces the curves of Magda's ears.

"To listen to God is not the same as to listen to the bumble bee or the squirrel. To listen to God is to turn your ears the other way." Her grandmother taps the centre of Magda's chest. "In here." One dewdrop trembles, collapses into a trickle. Magda's grandmother passes the back of her large paw across the thin black hairs, and all the dewdrops are gone. The black nose hairs quiver.

"Did I get borned from you or from my mother?" asks the little girl.

Her grandmother laughs. "Your mother gave birth to you, but you and me, Magda, we are a pair."

As she does every evening, Magda's grandmother shakes the fire in the wood stove with a coiled silver stick that looks like a bedspring. Then she gathers her granddaughter onto her lap. Resting both feet on the metal stand beside the stove door, she rocks. In her grandmother's arms, Magda learns the language of the fire, its sharp retorts and windy roars, its hissings and sputterings, its little shifts and settlings. Her grandmother tells about their ancestors around the fire of their night, how the animals stayed on the other side of the flames.

She tells about the sacred fire-tenders of old – how, to permit the fire to die was to allow the soul of the household to perish. She sings ancient tunes, her heart drumming beneath Magda's cheek, the tunes travelling through the child's ears and down to the special place inside her chest. Magda sleeps with her grandmother in the bed off the kitchen, coming half-awake every time her grandmother gets up to tend the fire, curling back into the circle of her warmth each time she returns.

On the last Saturday in August, Magda's mother arrives to take her daughter home. Mid-afternoon, everything loaded in the car, Susan hugs her mother and reaches for the tap on the kitchen sink. Just as her fingers touch it, she sees the eye. The long gleam of silver is not a tap, it is a fish. A dead fish. Susan shrieks and jumps back.

The eyes of both Magda and her grandmother turn into slits and drip tears of mirth onto their identical nubbin cheeks.

Susan and Dave Johnston are atheists. Dave is an optimistic man who prides himself on his logical mind and his powers of observation. There is little in the physical world that he does not notice, little that he cannot fix. Though he was raised in a devout family, religion now seems to him absurd, for the weak, those who go in for ouija boards, Tarot cards, that sort of thing. Dave is a tall man, and physically strong. He feels up to anything life could toss his way. With his brother, he owns a company that makes fine heritage furniture. Susan keeps the books.

Susan likes the sound of the sentence, "I am an atheist." She likes the slight tremor it tends to produce in her friends, even in the year 1993. She likes how it makes her feel about herself: finished with superstition, not in need of comfort, capable of making her own meaning. A business woman.

In the spring of 1984, when her son Peter was twelve years old, Susan had become pregnant again. When Peter was born, doctors had warned Susan against becoming pregnant again, later told her it would be impossible. Yet here she was. She had delayed telling her mother, although they talked on the telephone every Sunday afternoon.

"I have news for you," she said, finally, in early fall.

"I know already," her mother replied.

"You couldn't know this, Mom."

"You're pregnant."

"Now why would you say that?" Susan was so indignant at being robbed of her surprise that she wanted to deny her mother's words. "You know the doctors said I could never get pregnant again."

"The doctors don't know everything. My people told me. When I was out West this summer. You're going to have a girl." Susan's mother is part Blackfoot. Every summer she visits Alberta where she was raised, and stays with the Blackfoot relatives on her mother's side.

The amniocentesis had confirmed that the baby was a girl. Though she wanted a girl this time, Susan was annoyed. Again, her mother was right.

Dave shrugged. "What did she have to lose by making a guess? She had a fifty per cent chance of being right."

Three months before her due date, Susan and Dave had visited a Canadian Tire store to pick out paint. There, Susan had seen an entire wall filled with Cabbage Patch dolls. They were in tall, narrow boxes with cellophane fronts. There were dolls with every colour of hair and eyes. Every style of dress, sun suit, overall, sleeper. Near the end, half-way up, one of the boxes lay sideways. Susan moved closer. This girl doll was wearing a soft pink baby bunting with a hood pulled up over dark curls. The eyes of the doll were black, her cheeks as pink as the bunting. When Dave appeared, Susan took his arm.

"I'm going to get this doll for the baby."

Her husband shook his head. "Hold off on that, Sue. Cabbage Patch dolls are all the rage right now. By the time the baby's old enough to play with a doll, it'll be something else."

She knew he was right. This was the sort of sensible thing she would normally say.

She shook her head. "You're right about it being a craze that won't last, but I'm buying this doll, anyway." She heard her voice, wobbly with urgency.

Dave opened his mouth to speak, then stopped, and she saw that he was lumping her irrational desire with the fact that pregnant women get cravings – for pickles, for chocolate, for cleaning house. This was a temporary insanity that must be indulged: "Fine. Suit yourself."

In the car, she took the doll from its box and laid her cheek against the plush pink bunting. The wide black eyes stared into her own. Dave glanced over at her. She could feel the heaviness of his tolerance, could feel that at this moment she was not his mathematical wife, his business partner with the crackerjack mind, but "the little woman." She replaced the doll in its box and when they got home, stored it out of sight.

Until she gives birth to Magda, Susan Johnston has not thought of an ear as being beautiful; the ear holds for her vague connections to the illnesses of Peter's childhood. But her new baby's ears are exquisite, they are delicate shells, their curves sculpted, their flawless surfaces pellucid. Susan finds herself staring at Magda's ears as once, on vacation, she stared at the fragile beauty of the tiny shells on a beach in Atlantic Canada. And Magda is a peaceful baby, sleeping through the night at six weeks, napping both mornings and afternoons.

One afternoon in August when Magda is seven months old, Susan is in the laundry room ironing. An intercom connects her to the baby's second floor bedroom.

She likes ironing. Unlike most people these days, she hangs her wash outside to dry on the two long clotheslines Dave made for her shortly after Peter was born. She irons everything. As the iron passes over each item, it releases the scent of ivory snow innocence and the outdoors, the sun and the wind and the trees. As she irons, she enters a rhythm made of the sigh of the steam, the soft thud of the iron stood on end, the familiar, deft motions of reshaping the warm material under her fingers. When she is fully into this rhythm, she is deeply at peace, her mind, normally teeming with ideas and plans, empty and still.

Today she is near the end of the basket of flannelette diapers when an inner voice speaks to her. Afterwards, she will muse that it was like the voice that sometimes speaks clearly at the end of a dream.

Go upstairs and get the cabbage patch doll from the closet in the spare room and open the adoption papers. The papers will tell you who your daughter is.

Her peace dissolves and she comes to. It is a Wednesday morning in August; she's in her laundry room. Her grey-black hair is sticking to her forehead and her temples. She doesn't believe in inner voices, yet one has just spoken to her.

She switches off the iron and stands it upright, then climbs the stairs to the spare room looking in on the baby as she passes her door. Magda is on her back, deeply asleep.

In the spare room, she drags the box from the closet, opens it and takes out the doll in its pink bunting, along with the envelope containing the adoption papers. With the little scissors she uses to trim the baby's nails, she cuts the envelope. The doll's name is Clothilde.

Susan feels her crackerjack mind – so beloved of her husband – slowing down and seizing up. It is helpless before the paper she holds in her hand. Clothilde is the name of Susan's grandmother – her mother's mother who lived on the western plains.

That evening, when Dave returns from driving Peter to his baseball practice, she pats the stone step beside her. "Sit down for a few minutes, hon. I have something incredible to tell you."

Her husband puts one foot on the step, unties, then reties his running shoe. "Okay, shoot. I want to get the grass cut before I go back to get Pete."

She tells him about the inner voice, the name on the adoption papers of the doll she bought at Canadian Tire.

Dave Johnston straightens. He cracks his knuckles and shrugs. "Coincidence, Sue."

"But Clothilde was an unusual name for a Blackfoot Indian. It's an unusual name for a Cabbage Patch doll."

"Sure, that's what coincidence is. A phenomenon in which, for no reason, unusual things come together. I wouldn't give it another thought."

The next morning, Susan goes to the phone and dials her mother's number. Just as she is about to hang up, her mother answers.

"Hi Mom, it's me. Where were you?"

"Outside, whittling the willow. How's the baby?"

"She's fine. She, you're, not going to believe. What I have to tell you."

"Okay," says her mother. "I'm listening."

Susan tells about going to Canadian Tire, about the Cabbage Patch doll, the inner voice while she was ironing, the name on the adoption papers. Yes, says her mother, that's right, the baby is my mother. Clothilde.

"Mom, what do you mean, the baby is your mother? What are you saying?"

"The old ones told me. Last summer, when I was out there, when they told me you were pregnant with a girl."

"Mom, you never told me that."

"I don't tell you everything. Clothilde was a shaman to her people. I've told you that."

"Mom, this is ridiculous, this is, preposterous. How could Magda be Clothilde? I don't, Dave and I don't, believe in such things."

"That's why I didn't tell you."

Magda cannot bear the days of high wind. Wind howl blocks the sounds that weave the spell that holds her in her daily life, as the inner tepal of the lily holds the nectar. The sounds that make the spell: seed coats splitting beneath the soil of the south garden, bird beaks tearing strands of last year's grass, faint expanding crinkle of the honey locust leaves, whisper of earthworm bristles along soil-soft tunnels, unrolling fronds of emerald fern, tap of clematis on warm brick, cluck of the hummingbird, quiver of labellum as the bee alights. A high wind closes her up, imprisons her in its roar, leaves her deaf with the echo of its voice when it has died away. It is better when God breathes gently, His wind spirit a zephyr that enters her inner ear rhythmically, like the sea. As when she prays.

Magda spends the hour between eight and nine each evening on her knees, in her bedroom.

One evening, her mother appears in the doorway just as she finishes. "What is it you do, Magda, when you're on your knees?"

Magda sees that her mother's eyes are huge and black, that her hands tremble. The little girl opens her arms and steps forward. She

141

nestles her ear against the heart so sharp and rapid in her mother's throat. "Don't be afraid, Mom. On my knees, I'm listening. God is talking to me in His quiet voice."

Today the wind is high and Magda is happy when the muffled bell signals the end of recess. It is June of her grade three year, and Mrs. Gordon has assigned a composition. The instructions are printed on the blackboard. WRITE THE STORY OF THE MOST IMPORTANT EVENT OF YOUR LIFE SO FAR. REMEMBER, THE STORY MUST BE TRUE.

The class has been preparing for a week to write this story.

Magda picks up her yellow pencil and goes to the sharpener by the window. She likes the merry hollow grind as the shavings fall, the punch of fresh wood smell in her nostrils. Back at her desk, she bends over and begins. As she forms the round letters of her first sentence, the classroom vanishes and she is on the western plains in summer.

My Grandmother, Faun Skyefour, is half Blackfoot Indian. When I was four and a half years old, I travelled with my grandmother Faun to the west, to the place where my grandmother grew up and many people of the Blackfoot nation still live. We flew in a plane to Calgary, Alberta. From there we took a bus to Lethbridge, Alberta.

I sat in my grandmother Faun's lap. In the distance were mountains with silver tops. My grandmother told me that these are the Rocky Mountains. At the top of them is a different world with shining light, thin, air and a kind of time that lasts forever. Storms and rain and sunlight are born there, and many people have died trying to journey to the world at the top of the mountains.

We travelled through the fields of wheat that cover the plains. My grandmother, Faun, said that the wheat is like the sea, moving and dipping and rolling. She told me that before the wheat, there was grass. The grass fed the Buffalo its sweet green, and the Buffalo fed the grass with their droppings. The grass had deep roots that held the earth safe. My grandmother said that time is a circle and the time of the Buffalo will come again.

She said that Napi is the one who made this land. He shaped it, and in it we can see his body. We can see his rivers. My grandmother pointed to the river bottomlands. That is where the lodges of her people were set up in the winters.

My Grandmother Faun said that the grandfathers and grand-mothers, the old ones, the ones who lived here long before, can still be seen moving over this land by some people. Their voices can be heard at night and in dreams by those with good ears.

One morning, I finish my breakfast before everybody else and go outside. I skip along to where the rail fence begins and climb on. The fence is my horse, Dusty-Stocking. Today my uncle is going to teach me to ride. I can hold onto Dusty-Stocking only with the insides of my legs. I am not allowed to use my feet or hands.

Dusty-Stocking bucks, and I start to fall off, and I do fall off, right onto the hard dirt. Then I am screaming and screaming. My grandmother and uncle come running. They hold me and hug me and take me back to the house. They try to get me to drink water, but no matter what they do I am crying. Over and over they ask me what is the matter. I am not a crybaby and no bones are broken. Why am I hysteric?

The reason is that when I start to fall off the fence, I remember everything. I remember that I was alive before the old ones and I lived in this land Napi made. I fell off this same kind of fence, and a herd of shaggy animals trampled me, and I died. On that day I was wearing a top the colour of a deer, and when I hit the ground, the pushed-up sleeve of my top scraped right over my elbow. That was the last thing I saw before the big animals ran over me and I died.

I was four years old when I went to the western plains with my grandmother, Faun, and when I am four, I do not have the words to tell her why I am screaming and crying so long.

Susan raises her head. She has been away a long time, but Mrs. Gordon and Mr. McFadden are still sitting there. Still looking at her.

Her troglodyte tongue will not form a word.

She stands and walks out of the office, her daughter's story in her hand.

"Mrs. Johnston?" says Mr. McFadden.

She does not look back.

At dusk that evening, Susan Johnston picks up her daughter's composition and the old *Saturday Night* she brought home from the dentist's that morning. She steps into her backyard carrying a cup of hot tea along with the papers. The feeling has come back into her face and her jaw is tender. There is a smell of new, mown grass. She sits at the picnic table and smoothes the crumpled paper flat. She reads her daughter's story again. Her eyes dwell in every loop and line of the words: *I remember that I was alive before the old ones and I lived in this land Napi made.*

She opens the torn magazine and finds her place, re-reads the sentence by Robert Fulford: "They weren't prepared . . . for the arrival in their midst of Glenn Gould: it was rather like having a mountain range appear suddenly in the backyard."

She sets the papers aside, takes a sip of tea. In that instant, she understands that the mountains will not care about the little lives of Susan and Dave Johnston.

The Crystal Bowl

"If one carries the beast in one's guts, there is
no alternative, one has to give it everything."
— *Margio Vargas Llosa*

*W*e do this every so often, Rachel and Lynn and I. Rent a movie on a Friday night and banish Jed to the attic. Rachel, Lynn and I are women of a certain age. That means nobody needs us anymore. One life seems to have ended. We're free to discover a new fate, the one that belongs to the second half of our lives.

Each of us has her place on these film evenings. Lynn sits at the far end of the green couch. She controls the switch for the gas fire. Rachel sits at the other end of the green couch. She controls the lamp and the remote control. I sit in the middle. I have all the control I need. It's my green couch, my gas fire, my banished husband.

This Friday evening, we rent an Altman film, *Cookie's Fortune.* Near the beginning of the film, the wicked sister goes to her Aunt Cookie's heritage home to borrow a crystal bowl. No one answers when she calls "hello." She finds the bowl, then wanders through the house, finally discovering her elderly Aunt's body in an upstairs bedroom. At the moment of seeing the corpse, gun still in its hand, the wicked sister drops the crystal bowl. It shatters. She removes the gun, chews up the suicide note, and swallows it, determined to cover up the shameful way her Aunt has chosen to die.

When the film is over, Lynn has an orange and Rachel has an apple. I have a cup of chai tea. We discuss the film.

Then Lynn says, "A crystal bowl would never break like that, you know. They're really strong."

Rachel nods, and I add, "That's right. I have a crystal bowl. Jed's mother gave it to me when Jed and I were married. The bowl was in their family for generations. I've dropped it on the dining room carpet and I've dropped it on the kitchen linoleum, and it's never broken."

This is a boast, for I say it with an underlying pride in my carelessness, pride in what I can get away with, pride that I have more important things on my mind than taking care with a family heirloom. My pride is a river running below the surface of what I'm telling Rachel and Lynn.

The next evening Jed and I go to a pot luck dinner. At the dinner is a lion tamer.

This is unusual in itself. Jed and I do not move in circles that include lion tamers. We're teachers. Jed has rimless glasses, a chubby figure, grey hair. I have dyed red hair and I've kept my figure, more or less. Our friends tend to be quiet, bookish. They, and we, live safe, secure, predictable lives in the outer world; it's in the inner world that we find our excitement and our passions.

The lion tamer is at the party because the host's first cousin is visiting unexpectedly this weekend. The cousin, Emory Williams, who's from Houston, is writing a book on the circus. Emory is a tall, thin man with a tiny bristle moustache and shrewd brown eyes. He's travelled with a circus for months and now he's on his way home. The lion tamer is with him; I'm not clear why. Something about seeing a specialist in Houston.

The lion tamer's name is Mr. Xerxes Chaffinch. "Commonly known as Mr. X," says Emory Williams, as he introduces Jed and me. Mr. X extends his hand. I notice that his nails are long. When I see long nails on a man, I wonder about his sex life. Whether he has

How does a finger with a nail that extends beyond the pad of the tips negotiate the tender tissues of the vulva, the vagina? There are reddish-gold hairs on the backs of Mr. X's hands and on his forearms.

After we're introduced, Jed stands talking to Mr. X and Emory. I accept a glass of chilled white wine from the hostess and move over to stand near the fire while I sip it. From there, I study Mr. X.

The lion tamer is elderly, but his slim physique gives a first impression of a younger man. His hair is a matte brown, edged with orange-gold. It's not the roots that are orange, it's the opposite ends of the hair. It looks as if the brown hair has flames nibbling at it, as if the flames could at any moment rush the length of the hair and consume it. The lion tamer's eyebrows are a dark brown, obviously pencilled on. Again, there are orange hairs at the edges, as if a brown magic marker has been used to colour over orange eyebrows and has missed some of the hairs at either end.

At dinner, I maneuver myself into sitting across from the lion tamer. I want to talk to him. The people I know spend large amounts of energy and ingenuity to keep themselves safe from the terrors of the world; they acquire house and collision insurance, they go for annual checkups, take vitamins, drink bottled water. Here is a man who chooses to risk his life every day. His terrors are not the imagined specters of the future that trouble people like me; they are real terrors of the outer world. Ferocious beasts.

We settle ourselves, and Jed, who is beside me, makes small talk across the table with Emory. During a pause, I lean forward and look into the lion tamer's light blue eyes. "If I went into a cage with a lion and a tiger, what would happen to me, Mr. X? If I went in there tomorrow, say, with no training?"

"You'd be mauled. Killed, probably." Mr. X smiles as he says this, and smoothes back his two-toned hair.

"How come you aren't? Emory says you've been doing this all your life."

Mr. X accepts a basket of rolls from Emory, who is on his left. He takes one and puts it on his plate. "I understand the animals," he says, simply, breaking the roll in half. "I understand what's going on in their heads."

Jed's colleague, Marcia, is on Mr. X's right. Marcia has greasy brown hair. She smells of sweat. She doesn't believe in deodorant. Jed was on the committee that hired her. Some of them didn't want to hire her because she smelled. Some of them thought that shouldn't make any difference. She got the job, just barely. At a patio party in the summer, she'll raise both arms and lace her hands behind her head, exposing her hairy armpits for all to see. The other women on staff are shaved and waxed and plucked, trying, I guess, to forget that they're mammals. They talk behind Marcia's back. Half the time, she's left out of social evenings like this one. I'm waxed and plucked, like the others, but I'm happy when I see Marcia sit down across from me. She accepts the basket of rolls from Mr. X and smiles at him. There's a gap between her front teeth.

"Are you near the end of your career, Mr. X? Have you had enough of those cages?"

"Lion tamers don't retire, Ma'am." Mr. X shakes his head as he slathers his roll with butter; the orange hairs on the backs of his hands gleam in the candle light. "Lion tamer isn't my job, it's who I am. You can't retire from your life. Lion tamers die working. Clyde Beattie had a heart attack in the ring."

Marcia shakes her shoulders and her arms, rearranging them inside her sweater. She shifts her whole body so that she is facing Mr. X. She moves her shoulders again as if she's stroking her green sweater from the inside, with her skin. "So tell me, Mr. X. What is it that stands between you and certain death, when you go into that cage?"

Mr. X looks at Marcia with the same expression he has for all of us. He has the air of a man who's seen everything and come through; who holds a knowledge the rest of us don't have. Almost as if he pities you. No, not pity. You don't understand, you never will, but he's okay with that, too. That's the look on his face.

"Two things," he says to Marcia. "Two things stand between me and death. "My concentration. The stool."

"How's that?"

"Every time I enter that cage, I know that if I lose my concentration, even for an instant, I've had it. The beasts will know it and go for me."

Marcia nods and is silent for a moment, her eyes thoughtful. Then she tilts her head. "What about the stool?" she says. It's as if

Marcia can read my mind; she's asking the same questions I have. We exchange a little smile.

"The lion has one thing in his head. He smells me, he's looking at me, he's coming for me. I put up the stool with the four legs facing him. Now he has four separate points coming at him. His concentration is broken."

Mr. X has a look that's post-bitterness, I decide. His face tells me he's been caught in every hard place there is. He's railed against his fate. In the end, he's accepted it, come through on the other side.

"Did you ever lose your concentration, Mr. X?" I ask him.

"Once, many years ago." The lion tamer looks down at his plate. "I made the worst mistake there is." His head comes up and he meets my eyes. "I was pretty good back then, and I got cocky. Paid for it with three months in hospital. I went into hospital in Houston on January third and came out on April seventh. That was 1964."

We are silent. Mr. X's smile understands our incomprehension. Encompasses it. He picks up his full glass of water and drinks it all. His Adam's apple bounces up and down in time with his gulps. Under his chin is a tiny patch of orange-gold hair that the razor has missed.

When he puts down his glass, I ask him one last question: "How old were you when you decided to be a lion tamer?"

Mr. X shakes his head. "Oh, I was born wanting to be one. As soon as I was old enough to know anything, I knew I was a lion tamer. It was the only life that was possible for me."

Marcia lays down her knife and fork. She rests her chin on her hand, lets her little finger slide into her mouth, where it picks at her teeth. "How do you explain such a thing?" she exclaims, through her finger.

Mr. X smiles again. That same smile, from the other side of bitterness. "That's just the way it was."

On the way home that night, in the car, it's the lion tamer I want to talk about. "Just imagine how it would be," I say to Jed, "to have *that* as your fate. What a calling, what a *daimon!* That every day of your life you feel compelled to walk right up to Death, so close that his foul breath is what you're breathing, and he could kill you with one swipe." I shake my head. "A *daimon* that's so demanding there's no room for anything else in your life. No wife, no children, nothing. Just you and your phenomenal concentration."

A gentle spring rain has begun as we drive across the city towards home. Jed puts the windshield wipers on slow speed and their quiet rhythmic click is added to the swishing sound the tires make on wet pavement. I turn towards my husband: "How come Rachel and Lynn and I, and most other people, have such ordinary fates – having our children and raising them, doing our little jobs – while Mr. X gets handed one like that?"

Jed stops for a red light. He looks over at me and raises his shoulders in a monumental shrug.

That was Saturday evening. The next day, at noon, I break the crystal bowl that was given to me as a wedding present by my mother-in-law, the bowl that has been in my husband's family for generations.

The crystal bowl is sitting at the end of the kitchen counter. It's filled with fruit. I'd put it out the weekend before when we had company.

I break it with the leg of a stool. I'm holding the stool with my right hand, carrying it high in the air above the counter, when one of the four legs catches the bowl. Catches it, flips it into the air, and dashes it on the beige, linoleum floor. It shatters into hundreds of pieces.

The sun had come out just before noon, and I'd asked Jed if he wanted to go for a walk.

"I *am* going for a walk in half an hour," he said, "but I don't want you to come. You can't keep up. I'm going for the exercise."

Years ago, Jed used to get mad at me because we'd go on walks and I'd walk so fast he couldn't enjoy himself. He claimed my fast walking revealed a fault in my nature: I was driven, I couldn't relax. Nowadays, I've slipped from Type A to Type B and acquired a bad knee, whereas Jed has become focused – on daily exercise and keeping his heart rate up.

I got ready to go on my own. At the back door, I realized Jed wouldn't know whether to lock up, wouldn't know whether I'd taken my keys. I went to tell him, but he was in the bathroom, the fan on.

Jed hates for me to yell at him when he's in the bathroom. I decided to leave him a note. But Jed doesn't always notice notes, so I decided to put the stool at the back door, the note lying on top. He'd have to notice it to get outside.

That's how I came to be carrying the stool from one end of the kitchen to the other, past the counter where the bowl reposed in its intricate beauty. I could have dragged the stool; it has rubber feet. I could have lifted it slightly off the floor. There is no reason that I know of for me to have carried the stool high in the air, legs first, as if I were going forth to meet a lion.

When the crystal bowl falls on the floor and breaks, I yell for Jed to come out of the bathroom.

"What's the matter?" he says. He's half shaved, the hairy, soapy, straight razor still in his right hand. I point at the floor.

"For God's sake! How did you do that? That was my mother's crystal bowl."

The further in time we get from Jed's mother, living person, the more she metamorphoses into someone Jed can revere. People don't change only in life, me becoming dreamier and Jed becoming focused. They go on changing in death.

Jed is angry that I've broken the bowl. I'm angry that he's angry. I want him to sympathize with my distress.

"I'm going for my walk," I tell him. I pick up my keys, rattle them noisily, and exit by the back door.

Jed's mother was such a stickler for manners that to this day Jed can't remember which side of a dinner plate the knife and fork belong on. He refuses to use a serviette to keep his mouth clean when he's eating, won't stand up when he's introduced to a woman, won't wear a tie. His mother called me "dear." "Oh, you're such a dear little thing!" she'd exclaim in the middle of a conversation. I would squirm internally and feel like belching, or exposing a hairy armpit. Not that I had one to expose. I was as perfumed and nail-polished and de-haired as she was.

When she gave me the crystal bowl, she told me how valuable it was, how it would be my starter piece. I could add more crystal to the table as I could afford it, she said, her eyes coming to rest on the button I'd sewed back on my sweater with thread that didn't quite match.

Over the years, I would bring out the crystal bowl when we had company. One June, we had company from France. I filled the bowl with water and floated antique roses on the water's surface. Their elegant forms were set off by the crystal; their exquisite scent flavoured our days. The French were duly impressed.

When I get back from my walk, Jed is away on his. I kneel on the kitchen floor and begin carefully to lift the larger pieces of broken crystal into a paper bag. The third piece reaches out and stabs my finger, swiftly and surely.

My blood runs freely over the glittering crystal shards. The bleeding is copious. I attempt to staunch the flow, but it swiftly turns the Kleenex red; it seems a miniature blood river on its way to the Red Sea. Kneeling there on the kitchen floor, I begin to feel as if I'm in a fairy tale instead of my real life, as if I'm caught up in a series of predetermined events. The events have a pattern, but not one that I am permitted to understand. Not a logical "A follows B" pattern.

The pattern is broken crystal bowl Friday night, broken crystal bowl Sunday at noon; lion tamer's stool Saturday night, lion tamer's stool Sunday at noon. The inexplicable, close-in-sequence appearance of two things that it would be unusual to have appear once in any given weekend of my life. Will the next step be that I'll fall asleep for one hundred years?

Rachel and I have coffee at the Second Cup late Sunday afternoon.

"Turn it," she says. "Turn it round and round. Examine it as you'd examine a piece of crystal. At each turn, it'll reveal a different facet."

I've just finished telling her the story of my weekend, how nonplussed I am. How it has to mean something, but I can't see it.

"Turn it?" I repeat, stupidly.

"Just live with it," she says, her hazel eyes alight with the puzzle. "In time, it will give up its secrets." She smiles and her eyes change in their depths from shadow to sun dapple.

The couple at the table beside us laughs and the man reaches across and takes the woman's hand. Rachel and I come here for the atmosphere that envelops you the minute you walk in the door –

warmth, the aroma of fresh coffee, murmur of friendly conversations, Mozart coming from the speakers.

I look at my friend's fingers, how they broaden at the tip, then raise my eyes to hers. "I'm . . . different, Rachel."

Rachel crumples her napkin and puts it into her empty cup. She smiles at me and tilts her head. "Different?"

"Since I met the lion tamer. Something . . . something's coming to the surface."

"What kind of a something?"

I shake my head. "I'm . . . not sure. Something . . . big. I can tell you that much."

I bend down and lift my carry bag off the floor. From the jumble of books and papers protrudes a sharp point.

"Oh my God," exclaims Rachel, "you brought it with you? I hope you wiped off the blood!"

Slowly I draw out the long shard that cut me and hold it up to the light. Rachel leans forward, and the two of us stare for a long moment at its planes.

Elegant, self-contained, the pattern of a star on its surface. Razor-sharp. Translucent yet utterly opaque.

Acknowledgments

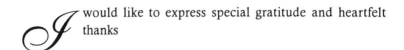 would like to express special gratitude and heartfelt thanks

to everyone at Boheme Press, particularly Max Maccari

to the writers and editors who encouraged, mentored and/or published my fiction from the beginning: Diane Schoemperlen, Patricia Abrams, Michael Carbert, Ian Colford, Gerard Dion, the Foxglove Collective of Kingston, Ontario, Jan Geddes, Joy Gugeler, Geoff Hancock, Joan Harcourt, Steven Heighton, Don McKay, R. W. Megens, John Metcalf, Bruce Porter, the Room Of One's Own Collective, George Sanderson, Kerry Schooley, James Strecker, J. R. R. (Tim) Struthers, Royston Tester

to Hamilton writers, especially J.S. Porter, Linda Frank, Rosalind Grant, Bernadette Rule, John Terpstra

to colleagues, supporters, researchers and readers at the Hamilton Public Library and the Hamilton Poetry Centre who are too numerous to mention by name and to Carol Bly (Letters from the Country) for the concept of the pond of rotting culture grief

to the Hamilton and Region Arts Council

to the staff of Bryan Prince Bookseller: Bryan Prince, Nancy McKibbin Gray, Tracey Higgins, Kerry Cranston, Cori Marvin, and to local author librarian, Beth Robinson

to my family, immediate and extended, especially my sister Marie Gear and my husband Dan Pilling without whom there would be no book

to my parents, Jean and John Gear: 1918 – 1999

About the Author

*M*arilyn Gear Pilling began writing in mid-life. In the past ten years, her poetry and stories have been published in many of Canada's literary magazines, broadcast on CBC radio, and have won several national awards. Her stories were featured in Oberon's *Coming Attractions* Series in 1995. In 1996, her first collection of short fiction, *My Nose Is A Gherkin Pickle Gone Wrong* was published by Cormorant Books to rave reviews. She has been Head of the Arts Departments at Hamilton's Central Library and currently is writing book reviews and community editorial board essays for the Hamilton Spectator and teaching Creative Writing at McMaster University. Pilling has a B.A. in English Language and Literature and a Masters of Library and Information Science, both from from the University of Toronto. Her first book of poetry, *The Field Next to Love*, will be released by Black Moss Press in Fall 2002. She lives in Hamilton and is currently at work on a novel.